"I'm not the kind of person men want to marry."

"You're not?" Kyle's eyes did a head-to-toe scan of her. "Why?"

"I'm not pretty," Sara admitted, embarrassed. "I don't know anything about fashion or how to dress. I certainly don't know anything about love or, uh, romance. I've never even dated."

"Sara, not every man is concerned about glamour or looks. Not that you have to worry. You're a very beautiful woman." He touched her arm as if to reinforce his words. "But what matters most is that you have a generous, tender heart that cares for people. That's the most attractive thing about you."

Inside her heart the persistent flicker of admiration she always felt for him flared into a full-fledged flame. But Sara didn't know how to respond. If she wasn't careful, his kindness would coax her into confessing the ugliness of her past and then he'd see that she wasn't any of those things he'd said.

LOIS RICHER

began her travels the day she read her first book and realized that fiction provided an extraordinary adventure. Creating that adventure for others became her obsession. With millions of books in print, Lois continues to enjoy creating stories of joy and hope. She and her husband love to travel, which makes it easy to find the perfect setting for her next story. Lois would love to hear from you via www.loisricher.com, loisricher@yahoo.com or on Facebook.

North Country Hero
Lois Richer

HARLEQUIN® LOVE INSPIRED®

Recycling programs for this product may not exist in your area.

 ™ LOVE INSPIRED BOOKS

ISBN-13: 978-0-373-81716-0

NORTH COUNTRY HERO

For Jehovah hears the cries of his needy ones
and does not look the other way.
                    —*Psalms* 69:33

I wrote this story after losing my father last September.
I dedicate this book to his memory.
I love you, Dad.

Chapter One

"I've already told you, Marla. I don't want to get involved with this 'Lives Under Construction' place."

The anger in the man's voice and the mention of her new employer piqued Sara Kane's interest so much, she stopped reading her book on the northern lights.

"Yes, Marla," he said with a weary sigh. "I know you told me I need to get involved, that you believe it will facilitate my recovery. And I will get involved. Eventually. But I told you I'm only going back home to Churchill to settle things. I'm not looking to get involved and I'm certainly not staying."

Sara suddenly realized she was listening in on someone's private cell phone conversation. Shame suffused her, but it wasn't as if he was whispering!

Sara tried to refocus on her book but couldn't because he was speaking again.

"Fine," he agreed with some exasperation. "I

promise you I will touch base with Laurel Quinn while I'm there, since you've already told her I'm coming."

Did that mean this man knew Laurel? Maybe he, like her, was one of Laurel's former foster kids, Sara mused.

"But touching base is all I'm going to promise you, Marla. You've been a wonderful therapist, and I appreciate everything you've done for me. But I have to stand on my own two feet now." Though he barked out a laugh, Sara heard an underlying bitterness. "Two feet—get it? That was supposed to be a joke."

Sara didn't understand what was so funny, but then that wasn't unusual. At twenty-two, there were a lot of things she didn't understand. But she would. She was going to Churchill, Canada, to work, but while she was there she intended to do all the things she'd missed during the ten miserable years she'd been in foster care.

First on her to-do list was finding her birth mother.

"I don't know what my future plans are, Marla. That's what I need to figure out." The man's voice suddenly dropped. "Everything I loved doing is impossible now."

The words brimmed with such misery, Sara had to force herself not to turn around and comfort him.

Don't give up, she ached to tell him. *Life will get better.*

"You're breaking up, Marla. I'll call you after I get to Churchill. Bye."

Churchill, Manitoba. Her new home.

A wiggle of satisfaction ran through Sara. This was her chance to start over. This was her opportunity to figure out how to be like everyone else instead of always being the oddball, and how to have the life she'd dreamed of for so long. Most of all, it was her opportunity to find the love she craved.

For Sara, Churchill would be a beginning. But for the man in the seat behind her, it sounded as if Churchill was going to be an ending. She couldn't help wondering why.

The train rumbled along. People went to the dining car to eat their dinner. Forewarned by Laurel, Sara had brought along a lunch so she could save her money. The thermos of homemade soup was warm and filling. She'd just sipped a mouthful when *he* rose behind her. His hand pressed the seat back near her head, dragging on it as he stood. A moment later he walked past her down the aisle, paused politely for a woman with a child to precede him, then followed her into the next car. Sara's curiosity mushroomed.

When the angle of his body and the dim overhead lights didn't give her a good view of his face, Sara decided she'd pay more attention when he returned.

That way she could ask Laurel about him when they arrived in Churchill.

But though she waited long hours, the man did not return. Frustrated that her formerly fascinating book on the northern lights no longer held her attention because *he* kept intruding into her thoughts, she finally exchanged that book for another in her bag, a romance about a hero determined to find the love of his life, who'd disappeared five years ago.

Yet even that couldn't stop Sara's mind from straying back to *him*. He was returning to Churchill. Because someone he loved had lived there, someone he'd had to leave behind? For a while she let the romantic daydream she'd been reading become his story. What would it be like to be loved so deeply that someone actually came to find you?

The train seemed to hum as it rolled along the tracks. Outside, darkness began to drape the landscape. Weariness overcame Sara. She leaned back to rest her eyes and again her thoughts returned to him. She'd heard deep longing in his voice when he'd mentioned settling things, as if he ached for someone.

Sara didn't understand a lot of things, but she understood that feeling.

She ached, too, for somebody to love her.

Maybe, just maybe, she could find the love she sought in Churchill.

* * *

"Churchill, Manitoba. End of the line."

Kyle Loness grimaced at the prophetic nature of the conductor's statement. This seemed like the end of the line for him, for sure.

He peered out the window, waiting for everyone else to leave before he rose and reached for his duffel bag. The bed in his sleeper hadn't afforded much rest. Now the bag's extra weight dragged on him, making his bad leg protest as he went down the aisle to the door. He winced at arrow-sharp stabs of pain. Though it felt as if there were still glass shards in his calf from the explosion, he knew that was a mirage.

He knew because there were no nerves below his knee. In fact, there was no leg. A prosthesis allowed Kyle to walk. Yet the phantom pains were very real, and for a moment, just before he stepped onto the platform, he wished he'd downed another pain pill.

"Can I help you?"

The whisper-soft query came from a young woman dressed in clothes clearly inadequate for this place. Her long caramel-brown hair flew every which way, tormented by a gust of icy wind off Hudson Bay. Her gray-shot-with-silver eyes blinked at him, wide and innocent-looking between the strands. She shuddered once, before steeling herself against the elements.

"Thanks, but I'll manage." Kyle immediately regretted his gruff refusal as surprise flickered across her face. But she said nothing. She simply nodded once and waited for him to move.

To prove he was fully capable of maneuvering, Kyle stepped down too quickly. He would have toppled onto the platform if not for the woman's quick reaction. She stepped forward, eased her shoulder under his arm and took most of his weight as he finished his ungainly descent.

While Kyle righted himself, his brain processed several fleeting impressions. First, she seemed too frail to survive Churchill. Her thin face looked gaunt and far too pallid in the blazing sun. The second thing Kyle noted was that she jerked away from him as soon as he was stable, as if she didn't like him touching her.

Well, why would she? He wasn't exactly hunk material, especially not since a roadside bomb had blown off his leg and scarred most of the rest of him.

"Thanks," he mumbled, embarrassed that he'd needed her assistance.

"You're welcome." She didn't smile. She just stood there, watching him. Waiting.

Kyle turned away, pulled up the sliding handle of his suitcase and leaned on it. He needed a moment to regroup before negotiating the long walk through the old train terminal and down the street toward his dad's house.

Except—his breath snagged in his throat—his dad didn't live there. Not ever again.

A knife edge of sorrow scraped his already-raw nerves. Kyle sucked in a breath and focused on getting out of here.

There were taxis in Churchill—two of them. But he was pretty sure both would have been commandeered by the first people off the train. He could wait for them to come back, but the thought of doing so made him feel as though he couldn't rely on himself. He'd grown up learning how to be independent and he wasn't about to give that up, despite his disability.

Kyle felt the burn of someone staring at him and knew it was her. The woman's scrutiny puzzled him. Once they glimpsed his ugly scars, once they realized he was handicapped, most people—especially women—avoided looking at him. She didn't. His surprise ballooned when her fingers touched his sleeve.

"May I know what happened?" she asked in that whisper-soft voice.

"I was in Afghanistan. I lost part of my leg." The words slipped out automatically. He steeled himself for the mundane murmur of *I'm sorry,* which everyone offered.

It never came.

"I'm so glad you're safe now," she said.

The compassion in her eyes stunned Kyle as much as the brief squeeze she gave his arm.

"God bless you."

God? Kyle wanted to snort his derision. But her sincerity choked his reaction. Why shower his frustration with God on her? It wasn't her fault God had dumped him.

"Thanks." Stupid that her fleeting touch should make him feel cared for.

Alone. You're alone, Kyle. Get on with it.

They were the only two people left on the platform. Kyle led the way inside the terminal. She held the door for him but he refused to say thanks again. He didn't want her help. Didn't need it. Coming here was all about taking back control of his life. About not being dependent.

On anyone.

"Hey, Kyle."

"Hey, Mr. Fox." Kyle added the traditional Native greeting in Cree then waved his hand at the stationmaster he'd known since he'd moved here when he was ten. He ordered himself not to wince when the old man ogled his scarred face. *Get used to it,* he told himself. Folks in Churchill weren't known for their reticence.

"What was that?" The young woman stood next to him, her head tilted to one side. "Those words you said?"

"That was Cree, a Native language. It means

something like 'How goes it?'" Kyle kept walking, pausing just long enough to greet his former school-teacher in French before moving on.

"How many languages do you speak?" the woman asked.

"A few," he admitted.

As a toddler, Kyle's first words were in French, thanks to his European mother. Then as a child, while his father consulted for the military, he'd become fluent in both Pashto and Dari. After that, learning a new language had come easily. In fact, his knack for languages was what had changed Kyle's status from reservist to active duty, and sent him to Afghanistan two years ago.

"It must be nice to speak to people in their own language." The woman trailed along beside him, held the station door open until he'd negotiated through it, then followed him to the waiting area out front.

"Yeah." He glanced around.

The parking lot was almost empty. Trains came to Churchill three times a week—often not on time, but they came. Natives of the town were used to the odd schedule and disembarked quickly after the seventeen-hour ride from Thompson, anxious to get home as fast as they could.

Tourists usually took longer to figure out the lay of the land. Local businesses got them settled, signed them up for some excursions if they could and fed them. Churchill made a lot of money from tourists. Except that somehow Kyle didn't think the woman behind him was a tourist, he decided after taking a second look. It seemed as though she was looking for someone.

So who was she?

Once Kyle had known all the town regulars. But he hadn't been home in two years, and a lot of things had changed. Things like the fact that his dad was never again going to stand beside him while they watched a polar bear and her cubs play among the ice floes in the bay.

Dad was gone and Kyle was damaged goods—too damaged now to scout the back country, climb the rocky shore or do anything else requiring intense physical effort. He wasn't even sure he could manage the walk home.

He paused to reconnoiter while his hand massaged his hip, as if it could short-circuit the darts of pain now shooting upward.

"Is something wrong?" Her again. Her quiet question was neither intrusive nor demanding. Just a question.

"Nothing's wrong." Kyle grimaced. Again he sounded sharp, irritated. He didn't mean to, but the rawness of the place matched his mood. Still, he'd better get rid of that chip on his shoulder. This woman was not his enemy. "I'm fine. Thanks."

"Okay." That calmness of hers—where did it

come from? What made her so accepting, so gentle in the face of his irritation?

None of your business. Stop thinking about her.

But he couldn't because the soft slap of her sneakers against the pavement told Kyle she was right behind him.

"Are you following me?" he asked, turning to stare at her.

"Sort of." The wind had tinted her cheeks pink, but now the color intensified into a rose blush. "Someone was supposed to pick me up." She checked the plain watch around her too-thin wrist.

Kyle thought he glimpsed the faint white mark of a scar, but then it was gone as she shifted her small overnight bag from one arm to the other.

"I'm late and they're not here."

"Stay here. They'll come to the station for you. Everyone in Churchill knows when the train comes in." He studied her again, curious about this waif-like woman. "Who are you waiting—?"

"Sara!" The yell came from a blond-haired woman who screeched her van to a halt, jumped out and rushed over from the parking lot. "I'm so sorry I'm late." She flung her arms around the younger woman in a bear hug. "Welcome."

"Thank you." Those silver-gray eyes grew shiny. Tears? Why? he wondered.

"You must be Kyle Loness. Marla told me you

were coming." The new arrival laid a brief hug on him, too, then laughed. "Welcome to you, too, Kyle."

Oddly enough the embrace felt good, even though it knocked Kyle slightly off balance.

"Thanks. I'm guessing you're Laurel Quinn." He smiled when she slid an arm around Sara's waist and planted a hearty kiss on her cheek in the same way his mom had done to him before cancer had sapped her strength. "You're the woman who's starting the youth center, right?"

"That's me. I see you know Sara." Laurel glanced back and forth between them.

"Uh, not really," he said, suddenly too aware of the younger woman standing silent, watching him. "We just got off the train together."

"Well then, Sara, meet Kyle Loness. Kyle, this is Sara Kane. She's going to be our cook at Lives Under Construction." Laurel beamed as she proudly said the name.

"Lives Under Construction," he repeated, remembering his conversation with Marla. "What exactly is that?" he asked, and immediately wished he hadn't. He didn't want to get involved.

"It's an alternative approach to serving time for young offenders," Laurel told him.

"Here?" He glanced around, struggling to put together the few pieces Marla had given him. "You've made Churchill your base?"

"Yes. It's perfect. The boys can't run away because there is no place to run to. With our quarters outside of town, it won't be easy for them to create much mischief, either." Like him, Laurel didn't miss Sara's shudder. "It's cold out here and Sara's not dressed for this wind. Why don't you come with us, Kyle? You can see my project for yourself. I'll drive you home later."

Home. The word made his stomach clench.

"Kyle?" Laurel frowned at the long silence. Her gaze slipped to his leg. "Okay?"

"Yeah, sure."

But it wasn't okay at all. He'd had the prosthesis on for too long. His stump was shooting pins and needles to his hip. He'd never make the walk to his dad's house in this condition. Might as well take the proffered ride and see what Laurel had created. There was nothing waiting for him at home, anyway. Not anymore. "I'd like to see your Lives Under Construction."

He didn't tell her he was also coming because he was curious about Sara, and her role in Laurel's center for troubled youth.

They walked together to Laurel's battered vehicle. Kyle took a second look at Sara, who shivered as the wind toyed with her coat. Ms. Kane didn't look as though she could survive a group of young offenders or the rigors of cooking for hungry teens.

Actually, she looked as if she needed another hug.

Don't get involved.

Despite the warning in his head, Kyle wondered what Sara's story was. He'd first spotted her yesterday when they'd boarded the train. During the ride he'd seen her twice more and thought she'd seemed a little tense. But she'd visibly relaxed the moment Laurel appeared and now gazed at her with a mix of neediness, adulation and hope.

Sara grabbed his bag and put it in the back of Laurel's van with her own small satchel. "You take the front." She waited until he had, then crawled into the seat behind. She remained silent as Laurel talked about her project. She didn't lean forward to hear. Obviously she knew all about the plans for Lives Under Construction. But then she'd have to if she was cooking there.

"We get our first six boys later this week." Laurel steered out of the parking lot and took a right turn. "A mix of twelve-and thirteen-year-olds."

Churchill's only highway ended about fifty miles out of town. Kyle knew they wouldn't go that far. Only the odd inquisitive tourist did that.

"None of these kids are model citizens." Laurel shrugged. "They wouldn't be in the system if they were."

He remembered that Marla had said Laurel was a former social worker. So of course she would know about the legal system as it related to kids.

"How long will they be here?" The pain in his leg was letting up but his mouth was dry from the medication he'd taken earlier. Kyle swallowed with difficulty, congratulating himself when it seemed no one had noticed the squeak in his voice.

Until Sara leaned forward and handed him an unopened water bottle. Whoever she was, this woman saw too much. Intrigued by Sara but also by Laurel's project in spite of his determination to remain detached, Kyle took a sip.

"Thanks," he muttered.

"You're welcome," Sara said.

"I have been given a one-year license." Laurel's pride was obvious. "If nobody messes up, the kids will be here for that long. I hope to get them excited about their education."

"Local school?" he asked, curious in spite of himself.

"Yes. As much as possible, I want them to become part of the community." Laurel hit the brakes to swerve around a red fox that raced across the road. She must have seen his grimace of pain as his shoulder bounced off the door frame. "Sorry."

"It's okay. Spring always brings them out." Kyle glanced around, noting the many signs of spring. New birth, new life. His dad's favorite season. His heart pinched.

"This is spring?" Sara hugged herself tighter into her thin coat. "It can't be more than a few degrees above freezing outside!"

"That's warm for Churchill in May." Kyle twisted

to look at her. "Enjoy it. When it gets hot, the bugs come out. That's not fun."

A tiny groan pushed through Sara's bluish-tinted lips before she subsided into silence.

When they finally pulled into the drive of a building that dated back to World War II, Laurel pointed out the renovations she'd incorporated into the old army barracks.

"It will do to begin with. Later I hope to expand and add on." She pulled open the heavy door. "Come on in. I'll give you both the grand tour. Then we'll have coffee."

Having gained respite from his pain during the car ride, Kyle followed Laurel and Sara into the massive structure, proud that he wasn't limping too badly and therefore wouldn't garner anyone's sympathy. He'd had enough sympathy for a lifetime.

"I'm impressed with what you've accomplished here," he told her, admiring the changes in the old building. It came as a relief to end up in the kitchen. He sank gratefully into a chair. "Really impressed," he added, noting the professional-looking kitchen. He was also aware that Sara had arrived before them and was now busy at the kitchen counter.

"Me, too." Laurel grinned.

"So this is your dream, to help at-risk kids. Marla said it's been a long time coming." He pulled his gaze away from the silent Sara and wondered at her deference to Laurel.

"Yes, it is my dream." Laurel's blue eyes grew misty. "This is a big answer to my prayers."

"Really?" She'd prayed to come to Churchill? Kyle bent forward to listen.

"Really." Her smile had a misty quality to it. "Just after our son was born, my husband was killed in a car accident. I was a single mom, alone and with a child to support." Her voice caught. "Brent was killed when he was sixteen, a victim of gun violence on the streets. His killer was thirteen. He'd been in the system for years, learned more violence with each visit."

"I'm so sorry," Kyle murmured, aghast.

"So am I." Laurel reached out and squeezed his fingers. "But Brent's death spurred me to a new goal. To create a place where young offenders could learn new ways instead of sinking deeper into violence. So here I am, almost fifty years old, starting a new career." She smiled.

"I'm glad." Kyle thought he'd never seen anyone who looked more at peace.

"Coffee?" Sara murmured from behind him.

Kyle tried to ignore the citrus scent that floated from Sara's hair directly to his nostrils as she reached to set a cup in front of him. Brief contact with her hand ignited a spark that shot up his arm.

Confused and irritated by the burst of reaction he did not want to feel, he edged away, shifting positions at the battered table.

"Thanks." He couldn't help the huskiness in his voice.

He did not like the reactions Sara evoked in him. When he'd been injured, his fiancée had flown to his side in Kabul. Repulsed by the extent of his injuries, she'd dumped him and left on the next flight. That still burned. No way was he going to let himself get involved again. Besides, he was only back in town to close this chapter of his life.

"You're welcome." Sara handed Laurel a brightly colored mug of steaming brew then sat across from Kyle in a prim position, feet together, back ramrod straight.

Sara hadn't poured a cup of coffee for herself. Instead, her long, thin fingers wrapped around a glass of plain water. Here in the kitchen, under the bright fluorescent lights, Sara might have passed for a teenager, except her serious eyes and the hint of worry lines around them told him she was older. Those eyes said she'd seen the rough side of life.

If Laurel had been a social worker, was Sara one of her "cases"? His questions about the younger woman mounted, matching the hum of the printer working overtime in Laurel's office around the corner. He studied Sara more closely. She didn't wear makeup. But then she didn't need it. She had a natural beauty—high cheekbones, almond-shaped eyes and wide mouth, all visible now that she'd scraped back her hair into a ponytail.

The room's silence forced Kyle to refocus. He realized that Laurel had asked him his plans.

"I'm inquiring because Marla suggested you might be willing to give us a hand. I thought perhaps you could teach my boys what living in the North Country means." Her smile flashed. "I've heard you're the best tracker these parts have ever seen."

Sara's unusual eyes widened and refocused on him.

"Was, maybe." Kyle grimaced at his messed-up leg then frowned at her. "Who told you about my tracking?"

"Everyone in town talks about you, Kyle. They're so proud of your service overseas." She went on to list all the things she thought he could teach her young offenders.

"Wait." Kyle had to stop her. "I wish you success, Laurel. But I can't take that on right now. Even if I could still do what I once did. Which I can't."

"I see." She didn't say anything more, nor did her face give away her thoughts.

Sara's forehead furrowed in a frown as if she had a question. But she didn't speak.

"And as for plans, I don't have any firm ones yet." He took a gulp of his coffee, glanced at his watch and knew he had to leave now, while the pain was still manageable. "I'm taking things one day at a time."

Just then a low, menacing rumble filled the room, followed by a loud pop.

"Oh, it's that dratted printer again. I'm beginning to wish I'd never seen the thing. It's become my worst nightmare." Laurel jumped up and raced to her office.

Sara's wide eyes met his. "Excuse me." She followed Laurel. It seemed as if she was eager to get away from being alone with him.

Kyle decided there was no point in sitting in the kitchen by himself. He walked to the office and paused in the doorway behind Sara, slightly shocked by what he saw. Two computers took up most of the floor space. They lay open, as if someone had been tinkering. A half-destroyed keyboard sat on top of a file cabinet beside a hard drive with six screws taped to it. In the corner, an assortment of cords and cables spilled out of a tattered cardboard box. He couldn't decide if someone was tearing apart PCs or putting them together.

"Can we do anything?" Sara asked after exchanging a tiny smile with Kyle.

"I have no idea what's wrong this time," Laurel said, glowering at the now-silent printer. "I suppose I'll have to call Winnipeg and get another sent out." She exhaled. "That will take at least three days."

"I can clean things up," Sara offered. "But I'd be no help with fixing anything electrical."

"I might be. My dad tinkered with computer stuff and I often helped him." The words poured out before Kyle could stop himself. "Want me to take a look?"

"Would you?" Laurel stood back. "It's jammed," she explained.

"Yeah, I see that." Kyle hid his grin as he eased past Sara. He pulled over an office chair and sank onto it, bending to examine the innards of the machine. With painstaking slowness he eased bits and pieces of paper free. After a moment of watching him, Sara brought a trash can so he could throw out the scraps. "Thanks."

She didn't smile, simply nodded. But those gray-silver eyes of hers followed every move he made between quick glances at the monitor. Since it was filled with an error message, Kyle couldn't figure out what was so captivating. He refocused on the printer, removing the ink cartridge and resetting it after he'd lifted out the last shredded bit of paper.

"She has quite a stack of paper here. Do you suppose she's printing a book?" he teased, winking at Sara.

"Sort of." Sara picked up one of the printed sheets and read it. "It looks like a list of rules and procedures at Lives Under Construction. Is there one for each boy?" she asked Laurel.

"Yes. I was hoping to have them done before the boys get here."

"Don't worry." Sara reached out and squeezed her fingers. Kyle noticed a smile flit across her lips. "I'm sure Kyle can do something. Can't you?" She looked at him with a beseeching gaze that made him want to fix this fast. Why was that?

"It's a good printer," he told them. "But it's touchy about loading in a lot of paper."

"I think I know what that means. You're not supposed to print more than a certain number of sheets at a time and then refill. Right?" She raised her eyebrows, waiting for Kyle's agreement.

"Yes. That would be a good idea. But for now this thing needs a new part before it will work again." He stood too quickly and clasped the corner of the desk to balance. A millisecond later Sara's hand was on his elbow, steadying him.

There it was again, that lightning-bolt reaction to Sara's touch. Kyle eased out of her grasp as fast as he could without looking rude.

"I suppose a new part will take forever to get here and cost the earth." Laurel sighed.

"Not necessarily. My dad used to have a printer like this." Kyle smiled at the memory. "Dad was a pack rat. I'm pretty sure the old printer is still in a closet somewhere. I could see if it's still there and strip the part for you, if you want." He didn't look at Sara. The flare from her touch still lingered on his skin.

"But you've just come home," Laurel said. "I'm sure you're tired."

"I'm fine." Not quite true but Kyle wasn't going to tell her that.

Laurel glanced once at the printer, her longing obvious. "Look, Kyle. I appreciate it, but—"

"Laurel, let him try," Sara urged.

"She's right," Kyle agreed, surprised by Sara's mothering tone. "Let me take a look at home first. If I can't find anything, then you'll have a better idea of your next step."

"See? That makes sense." Sara grinned at him as if they shared a secret and when she did, his heart began to gallop.

Kyle tried to ignore the effect this stranger was having on him.

"You're right. Thank you, Kyle." Laurel stepped forward and hugged him. "You are a godsend."

"I doubt that." He glanced toward the kitchen. "Do you mind if we finish our coffee before we leave? I haven't had coffee that good since I left home."

"That's Sara. She can make anything taste wonderful." Laurel led the way to the kitchen.

Kyle stood back but Sara, her cheeks now pink, motioned for him to precede her. Once he was seated, she poured fresh coffee. Then she sat with folded hands, listening intently as he and Laurel chatted, though she never offered her own opinion. Very aware of the way Sara kept glancing toward the office, Kyle figured she must be impatient to check her email so he finished his coffee quickly, almost scalding his tongue.

It was time to go home. Time to stop avoiding the truth.

Back in Laurel's car, Sara again sat in the rear seat but this time she leaned forward to listen as Kyle described Churchill's landmarks. Ten minutes later they arrived at his father's house.

"I'm sure you'd like a few moments alone," Laurel said. "I have some things to do downtown. We'll come back in half an hour. Will that give you enough time, Kyle?"

A lifetime wouldn't be enough to reconcile losing his father but all he said was "Yes. Thanks." He climbed out awkwardly.

In a flash, Sara exited the car and lugged his bag to the door.

"Will you truly be all right?" she asked, her somber gaze holding his.

"I'll be fine." He wanted to be upset at her for lugging his suitcase out, but her compassion was genuine so he forced himself to smile. "I'm used to managing."

"Okay." She opened her mouth to say something more, but apparently thought better of it because she turned around and climbed back into Laurel's car without another word.

Kyle waited until the battered SUV rumbled away. Then he faced the house.

Home. He was finally home.

He squeezed his eyes closed against the loss that burned inside.

Why didn't You take me instead? he asked God. *I'm useless, but Dad wasn't. He was needed around here. What am I supposed to do now?*

Kyle stood there, waiting. But no answer came.

He was all alone. He'd better get used to it.

He was strong, he was knowledgeable and he was kind enough to help when asked. But Kyle Loness made Sara daydream and she couldn't afford that.

Because of Maria.

"Sara? Are you awake?" Laurel shifted the van into Park then turned to frown at her. "Oh, you are awake."

"Yes." Sara shoved away thoughts of Kyle.

"Well, I'm going to be about fifteen minutes. Then we'll pick up a few groceries before we go back to Kyle's. Do you want to wait for me in the car?" she asked as she climbed out.

"No." Sara followed her onto the sidewalk. "I'd rather walk a bit. I need to stretch my legs."

"Okay. Stick to the main street. I remember your

skewed sense of direction," Laurel teased. "Don't get lost on your first day in Churchill."

"I'm better at direction now than I was." Sara blushed, embarrassed by the reminder of her first faux pas after she'd left foster care. "I won't get lost."

She waited until Laurel had entered the building before heading toward Kyle's house.

The thing was, no matter how Sara tried, she couldn't seem to forget about him, and not just because he was so good-looking. Good-looking? Her brain scoffed. Kyle Loness was heartbreakingly handsome. Tall and muscular, the faint shadow of a beard defined the sharp jut of his jaw. Sara supposed he grew it to hide the scar that ran from the outside corner of his eye straight down past his jawbone, which, in her opinion, did nothing to diminish his good looks. And when he'd looked at her with his cornflower-blue eyes, a funny little shiver wiggled inside her, just like the heroines in the romantic novels she loved. How silly was that?

But it wasn't only his good looks that drew her. The image of Kyle working on Laurel's printer had been burned into her brain. Obviously he knew about computers. And she didn't. But she could learn, if someone would teach her. Someone like— Kyle? Maybe he could help her find her family.

Sara scanned the street ahead and saw him standing where they'd left him. Her silly heart resumed the pattering that had begun when he'd stepped off the platform and stumbled into her arms. She tried to quell it by reminding herself that Kyle Loness would find little interest in her. Why would he? Sara knew nothing about men.

Is it only his computer knowledge that intrigues you?

Of course it was. He might look like a romance hero but Sara knew nothing about romance, men or relationships.

Confused by her thoughts, she refocused on Kyle, who seemed lost in thought. Then he straightened, stepped toward the house and jerked to a stop. In a flash Sara realized why. Kyle had forgotten about the stairs and was now trying to figure out how to maneuver them to get into his house.

She had a clear view of his face. The pain lines she'd glimpsed on the train when he'd hobbled to his seat this morning had now etched deep grooves on either side of his mouth. He bit his bottom lip, grabbed the railings on either side and basically dragged himself upward, inch by painful inch, increasingly favoring his injured leg. His chiseled face stretched taut with concentration as he fought his way upward. She held her breath, silently praying for him, only exhaling when he finally conquered the last stair.

When Kyle paused, chest heaving with his efforts, Sara wanted to cheer. The sun revealed beads of perspiration dotting his face. For a moment he seemed to waver, as he had when he'd stepped off the train and again earlier, in Laurel's office. Sara took an automatic step forward to help, but froze when he reached out and turned the doorknob.

This was his homecoming. He wouldn't want her there.

She didn't belong. Again.

Hurt arrowed a path through her heart. She squeezed her eyes closed.

Focus on why you're here, Sara. You're here to help the kids. To figure out God's plans for your future and to make up for Maria.

For years Sara had tried not to think about the little girl. But now, as she fingered the scar at her wrist, the memories burst free of the prison she'd locked them in.

She'd been twelve when she tried to escape her foster home, unaware that her foster sister had followed her onto the busy street—until she heard Maria's cry when the car hit her. Sara had rushed to the child, cradling her tiny body as life slipped away, unaware of the shards of headlight glass that dug into her wrists, left behind by the speeding car.

Sweet, loving Maria had died because of her.

In shock and overwhelmed by guilt, Sara had been too scared to tell police the real reason she'd run, so after she'd relayed all she remembered about the car that had hit Maria and received stitches on her wrists, they'd taken her back to her foster parents, the Masters. The couple used Maria's death to convince Sara that if she tried to leave again, her foster siblings would pay. After that, there'd been no need for the Masters to lock her in the basement each night.

Sara's overwhelming guilt kept her in their abusive home. She had to stay to protect the other kids, as she hadn't protected Maria. She'd stayed until her new social worker—Laurel—uncovered the Masters' perfidy.

Almost eighteen, Sara had finally been removed from their care. But she hadn't gone home because she didn't have a home anymore. All she had were faded memories of her mother sitting on the sofa crying and her father stoically staring straight ahead while strange people took her away from them. She'd never known why it had happened and she'd never seen her family again.

Now she needed answers.

Blinking away her tears, Sara watched Kyle disappear inside his house. She waited a moment longer, then walked back to Laurel's car, puzzling over why she'd felt compelled to ensure Kyle had made it inside his house.

"Because I saw how lost he looked," she whispered to herself. "Because he needs help. Because... I don't know."

"There you are." Laurel's gaze rested on Sara's hand as it rubbed her scar. She moved closer, touched a fingertip to the tear on Sara's cheek then wrapped an arm around her shoulder. "You've been thinking about the past again. Oh, my dear Sara. You're free. God has something wonderful in store for you. Don't let the past drag you down."

"No, I won't." Sara dredged up a smile, hugged her back then walked beside her to the grocery store. But as they strolled down the aisles, she thought of Kyle inside his empty house.

They had something in common. Both of them had lost their families and neither of them could just forget about it.

Maybe, somehow, she could help him get over his loss.

Maybe if she did, he'd teach her how to use a computer.

Maybe then she'd finally find her family.

Chapter Two

Kyle rubbed his eyes, unable to dislodge memories evoked by the familiar aroma of his home. Tanned leather and Old Spice—it smelled of Dad, of happiness, of moments shared together. All of which were gone.

Emotion rose like a tidal wave. He fought for control.

When Kyle was younger, Churchill had been a fantastic adventure he'd embraced. Now it was just another problem in his life.

But for a moment, as the midmorning sun warmed Kyle through the window, the sensation of being loved enveloped him. He relaxed into that embrace. Comfort erased the pain of loss that dimmed everything in his world these days.

Home—without his dad? He closed his eyes and wept.

Moments later, footsteps treading up his stairs

shattered his privacy. He rubbed his shirtsleeve across his face. The computer part. Of course.

"Come on in," he called before they could knock.

Laurel preceded Sara into his kitchen. "Do you need more time?" Laurel scanned his face, then the empty tabletop.

"I haven't looked yet." He tore his gaze from the wall where a family photo hung. It had been taken six months before his mom's death. "I was just sitting here—remembering."

"You can help us out another time, when you're more rested," Laurel said in a gentle tone.

"I'm fine." Kyle didn't want to give Laurel any more chances to draw him into her program at Lives. He'd do this one thing for her now and then get on with his own life. He opened a door that had once been a pantry and nodded. "Yep, just as I thought."

A small squeak of surprise made him glance over one shoulder.

Sara's eyes were huge. She met his gaze, looked back at the shelves and said, "Oh, my."

Finding her understatement hilarious, Kyle chuckled as he dug through his father's accumulation of computer parts. "I told you Dad was a pack rat."

"No luck, huh?" Laurel asked when he drew back from the cupboard.

"Not yet." Kyle motioned to Sara. "Could you help me for a minute? I think the printer is on the bottom of this shelf. If you could hold up this box

while I free it, I wouldn't have to waste time unpacking all this junk."

"Okay." She moved beside him and followed his
directions exactly.

With a tug Kyle freed the printer, but in doing
so brushed against Sara. Assailed by a host of reactions, from the fragrance of her hair to the way
one tendril caressed her cheek, to the fierce look
she gave when he had to yank on the cord to free
the end, he realized that asking for Sara's help had
been a bad idea.

He moved away, eager to put some distance between them and hopefully end his heart-racing response to her.

"Thanks." He set the printer on the table and
opened it.

"If you explained how to reinstall it, I wouldn't
have to drag you back out to Lives. Maybe I could
do it myself," Laurel said.

Kyle lifted his head and arched one eyebrow.
From what he'd seen in her office earlier, Laurel
Quinn's aptitude did not lie in computers.

"Yeah." Her face turned bright pink under his
look. Laurel laughed. "You're right. I haven't got
a clue."

"I can do it in a matter of a few minutes," he told
her as he lifted out the part she needed. He deliberately didn't look at Sara. "But you will have to
bring me back home after, and I know you're busy."

"I've got almost everything ready to greet the first two boys, Barry and Tony." Laurel's eyes shone with expectation. "I'm hoping that while you and I are busy with the printer, Sara will start some of her fantastic cinnamon buns for tomorrow."

"I can do that." Sara, cheeks pink, looked away from Kyle. What was that about?

"I've got what we need." He held up the tiny relay switch. "I'm ready to go."

"Oh, Laurel, I just remembered. We'll need to move those groceries so there will be enough room for everyone," Sara said quickly.

Too quickly? Kyle searched her face. A puzzled Laurel opened her mouth, but Sara grabbed her arm and pulled, insistent. Frowning, Laurel stepped outside.

"Come out when you're ready, Kyle," Sara said, her voice a bit forced. "We'll meet you at the car."

And that was when Kyle got it. Sara knew the stairs gave him problems. She was keeping Laurel busy so he could navigate without feeling as if they were watching him.

Her thoughtfulness eased the knot of tension inside.

Sweet, thoughtful Sara. Why couldn't he have met someone like her first?

Kyle shut down the wayward thoughts. He'd ruled out romance in Afghanistan the day he'd been dumped, and he wasn't going to change his mind now. Anyway, Sara couldn't care about him. How could she? He was a ruined shell with nothing to offer a woman. He couldn't even figure out his own future.

Kyle shrugged on his jacket, shoved the printer part in his pocket and stood. He'd get this done and then move on to his own business. Sara was nice, sure. But there was no point in pretending her kindness was anything more than that.

Self-consciously he tromped down the stairs and walked to the car. Once again, Sara was seated in the rear seat, so Kyle sat in front. Once again, he filled in the drive's silences with facts about Churchill. And once again, after he got the printer running, Sara served him her delicious coffee along with a sandwich and some kind of lemon cookie that melted in his mouth. As Kyle ate, he quashed his yearning to linger, to get drawn in by the warmth of Sara's smile and forget the emptiness that awaited him at home. He couldn't afford to forget that. His future wasn't here in Churchill. God had made sure of that.

So finally he pushed back his chair, thanked Sara for the lunch and asked Laurel to take him home. Sara walked with them to the car.

"I'm glad to have met you, Kyle," she said, hugging her arms around her thin waist, revealing the scars he'd noticed earlier. "I'll be praying for God to bless you with a wonderful future."

"Thanks." He wanted to tell her asking God for

anything was pointless but he didn't. Instead, as they drove away, he voiced the other question that plagued him. "What is Sara's story, Laurel? Why is she here in Churchill? She looks like she'll blow away in the wind."

"You'll have to ask Sara. Suffice it to say that she deserves happiness and I hope she'll find some here. She's a wonderful person." Laurel smiled at him. "So are you, Kyle. Anytime you want to fill in a few hours of your day, feel free to drop by. Lives Under Construction can always use another hand."

"I know Marla told you I'd be interested in doing that," Kyle admitted. "But the truth is, all I want to think about right now is cleaning up my dad's place."

Laurel patted his shoulder then swung the van into his driveway. "After you've had time to grieve, please visit us, even just for another cup of Sara's coffee."

"I'll think about it," Kyle said, knowing he'd do no such thing. He climbed out of the car. "Thanks again. See you."

Kyle waited till Laurel's car disappeared, then braved the stairs again. Inside, the house seemed empty, lonely. He flicked up the thermostat and sat down in his father's recliner in the living room. A notebook lay open on a side table. He picked it up.

"Two weeks until Kyle comes home. Yahoo!" His father's scrawl filled the page, listing things they'd do together. Kyle slammed the book closed.

Why? his heart wept. *Why did You take him before I could see him again?*

Suddenly he heard Sara's words in his mind.

I'll be praying for God to bless you with a wonderful future.

Well, Sara could pray all she wanted, but whether God granted her prayers or not, nothing could make up for the loss of his dad.

With a weary sigh he rose and thumped his way to the kitchen, where he sat down to deal with the stacks of mail someone had dropped off. For a moment, he wished Sara was here with him. Somehow he thought that smile of hers and the calm way she approached life would make facing his not-so-wonderful future a whole lot easier.

But of course, imagining Sara in his house was just a silly dream. And Kyle was well aware that it was time he let go of dreams and face reality.

"Laurel, what's an ATV?" Sara shifted to allow the flames of the fireplace to warm her back.

"All-terrain vehicle. Like those big motorized bikes we saw this afternoon. Why?" Her friend stopped working on her sudoku puzzle to glance up.

"Kyle mentioned an ATV."

"Well, we have an ATV here," Laurel told her. "But I'm not sure you should try riding it without some lessons."

"I'm sure I can walk anywhere I need to go. I'm

looking forward to it." Sara loved to walk. In the time since she'd been released from the Masters' home, she'd discovered the freedom of going wherever she wanted, of turning around, of changing direction without having every movement scripted for her. That freedom was precious. Sara ignored Laurel's next remark about winter being too cold for much walking. "Tell me about Kyle's father."

"His name was Matt, ex-military," Laurel said. "I knew him a little—a very nice man, full of laughter. He and Kyle ran a tourist business together. Matt couldn't go overseas when Kyle got hurt because he'd had a heart attack. He didn't want his son to know. I think the hardest thing for Kyle to accept is that his dad isn't here with him."

"There's a kind of reverence in his voice when he mentions his father." Also an echo of utter loss that Sara couldn't forget. "He must have loved his dad very much."

Laurel stayed silent for a few moments "Sara, you're not comparing the love they shared with—Well, you don't think of your foster father as your dad, do you? Because the Masters are not in any way part of who you are. They tried to ruin you, but you were too strong. Now your heavenly Father has other plans for your future."

"I wish I knew what they were." Sara wanted to escape the misery she'd endured. But at night, when the darkness fell, those horrid feelings of being unloved returned.

Actually, they never quite left her. That was why she needed to find her birth family—to make newer, better memories.

"Hang on to the truth, Sara," Laurel told her.

"The truth?" Sara wasn't sure she knew what that was anymore.

"You are the beloved child of God. But you have to trust Him and be patient for His work to erase what the Masters did." Laurel got up to press a kiss against the top of her head. "I love you, too."

Sara squeezed her hand. But she waited until Laurel was busy making hot chocolate before she slid a sheaf of papers out of her pocket and studied them.

To find your birth parents we must have these forms signed and returned along with the fee and a copy of your birth certificate. This will initiate a search of our records.

So many times Sara had wondered about the mother who only came back to her in fragmented dreams. Who was she? Why had she put Sara into foster care? Why had she never come back? Didn't she love Sara? Didn't her father care that his daughter might need him?

In the past, Sara had come up with a thousand reasons why her parents had never come to retrieve her—fairy tales, happily-ever-afters, like the romance stories she loved reading.

But now she needed the truth. She wanted to find her parents, embrace them and let their love erase the past. She wanted to have what Kyle had lost— people who loved her always.

She wanted a forever family.

"Here you go, sweetie."

"Thanks." Sara hurriedly tucked her papers into her pocket before accepting the gigantic mug from Laurel. Laurel was as close to Sara's ideal mother-fantasy as anyone had ever been, but even Laurel couldn't fill her need for her mother's love.

"Enjoy it." Laurel smiled. "Savor this time alone because once the boys arrive it's going to get mighty busy." She sat in the chair across from Sara, her face serious. "Are you sure cooking here won't be too much for you?"

"I'm sure." Sara cupped her hands around her mug.

"Let me tell you a bit about each boy so you'll be prepared." Laurel gave a brief history, ending with the youngest and in Sara's eyes the most vulnerable boy, Rod.

"I think I'll like Rod." Sara knew she'd like all of the boys. Kids were easy to love.

"I'm not telling you about them because I expect you to get involved with their programs," Laurel said.

"Oh?" Sara frowned, confused.

"I hired you to cook for us because I know how

great you are at it." Laurel leaned forward. "But I want you to be free to do other things."

"Like what?" Sara already had a to-do list. Finding her family was first.

"Sara, you lost most of your childhood being a servant to the Masters. All the years you should have been a kid were spent making sure the other foster kids were okay."

"I had to do that," Sara said simply.

"You shouldn't have had to," her mentor insisted. "You're twenty-two. Have you ever taken time to think about yourself?"

"I managed." Sara didn't like to dwell on the past.

"Oh, my dear, you managed wonderfully. But now you have this time in Churchill and I want it to be your time. I want you to enjoy your life, find new interests. Make new friends." Laurel's voice softened. "I want you to focus on your future."

Sara thought about Kyle, alone in his house with that awesome yard. Rod would be arriving tomorrow. The sprout of an idea pushed down roots in her mind. She tucked it away until she could consider it more thoroughly.

"I will focus on my future. But I need you to do something for me, too, Laurel." Sara paused to assemble her thoughts. "I know I'm going to love it here. But I will only stay till Christmas. By then I believe God will have shown me what he wants me to do with my future."

"Well…" Laurel inclined her head.

"No, I mean it. I know myself, Laurel. I'll love it here, I'll get too comfortable and I'll want to stay. But you must ignore that, even if I ask you not to. You have to find someone else to take over for me after Christmas. Promise?" She leaned forward, her gaze intent on Laurel.

"If you insist," Laurel finally agreed.

"I do. I thought about this a lot while I was going to cooking school. Our minister said that in order to be the person God intends us to be, we must discover what He wants us to do." She leaned back, smiled. "That's what I am going to do while I'm here in Churchill. I'm going to search for God's plan for my future. So you cannot let me talk you into my staying."

Laurel studied her for a long time before she nodded. "All right."

"Now, what kind of things should I do while I'm here?"

"There's a pool at the recreation center attached to the school. You could take swimming lessons," Laurel told her. "Also, the school holds classes for anyone who wants to upgrade their education. You might want to look into that."

"Yes, I do." Sara didn't feel compelled to explain. Though the Masters had claimed Sara was home-schooled, Laurel had revealed their lies.

Laurel understood how awkward and geeky Sara felt, how much she wanted to shed her "misfit" feelings and be like everyone else. That was why she read so much. But sometimes it wasn't enough to just read about something. Her reaction to Kyle was a prime example. Nothing she'd read had prepared her for the instant empathy she felt for him.

"I'll pray that God will reveal His plans to you, Sara, so you'll be able to figure out what He wants for your future."

Sara already knew what she wanted in her future. She wanted her family reunited.

"Could I take computer classes?" Sara asked.

"Why not? You'll probably have to wait till fall for the new sessions, though. We'll phone and check tomorrow. I'll pray that God will reveal His plans to you so you'll be able to figure out what you want for your future." Laurel drew her into a hug.

She already knew what she wanted; she wanted her family reunited. But she closed her eyes and let her spirit revel in Laurel's embrace. Somehow that triggered thoughts of Kyle. Hugs were new to her, but he was used to them. He'd had parents who loved him and showed it. She'd seen it in the photos on his kitchen wall. He came from a tight-knit happy family.

"I'm going to bed now," Laurel said, releasing her. "You must be tired after that long train trip."

"Oh, no. Riding on that train was like being rocked to sleep." Sara could remember being rocked. Barely.

Laurel kissed her forehead. "Goodnight, sweetie."

"Goodnight, Laurel." Sara followed her, stepped into the room Laurel had given her earlier and gazed around. Her room. Space that belonged to her and her alone.

For now she had a home, just like Kyle.

Sara marveled at how far she'd come today. She loved Churchill from the moment she'd stepped off the train. Rough and wild, but brutally honest. Everyone seemed friendly—except for Kyle. An image of him sitting in his kitchen—exhaustion, agony and utter loss etched on his face—filled her thoughts. Sara could excuse his brusqueness because he'd been hurting, body and soul.

What she couldn't excuse was the way she'd stared at him so admiringly.

"Stop thinking about him," she scolded herself. "This isn't a fairy tale. He's a wounded veteran who lost his father. He's none of your business."

To dislodge Kyle's face from her mind, Sara curled onto the window seat, seeking the rolling ribbons of northern lights her book had talked about. But Laurel said the approach of summer meant it would stay light well into the night, that Sara wouldn't see the lights for months.

The northern lights, learning the computer—it

seemed as though everything had to wait till fall. But she would only be here till Christmas. Would she find her family by then?

She had to. As soon as possible.

Reading had always been her escape as well as her education, but Sara now knew book knowledge wasn't the same as actually living and experiencing. She was short on experience. That was why she always felt as if she was a step behind everyone else. But she would catch up; she would learn about love and families and all the things other people took for granted.

She tugged the papers from her pocket and began to fill them out. Tomorrow she'd visit Kyle, not only to discuss the idea she'd had earlier to help Rod, but because she didn't want to wait until fall to learn how to use a computer. Maybe she could persuade Kyle to do an exchange—she'd clean his house or maybe cook him something and he'd teach her how to use a computer to search for her family.

Because her family *was* out there. Somewhere. Sara just had to find them. Then she would finally have somebody who loved her, somebody she could love back. She'd have the circle of love Kyle had always known to support her in doing whatever God asked of her.

"Please help me." The prayer slipped from Sara's lips as she peered into the growing gloom. "Please?"

Chapter Three

"Thank you." Kyle paid the delivery boy, hefted the box of groceries onto the counter and closed the door. "Finally," he muttered.

He grabbed the tin of coffee, opened it and started a fresh pot of brew. While he waited impatiently he unpacked the rest, bumping into several pieces of furniture in the crowded room as he stored his supplies.

It wasn't long before exhaustion dragged at him, caused by staying up too late to open the cards and letters full of sympathy from those who'd known his dad. Kyle turned, swayed and grabbed the back of a kitchen chair to keep from toppling over. He needed to sit, and fast. But first he poured himself a cup of too-strong coffee.

"Better," he groaned, savoring the rich taste. "Much better." But not as good as the coffee Sara had made him.

Kyle pushed that thought away.

The prosthesis ground against his skin—his "stump," he corrected mentally. There weren't enough calluses to protect the still-raw tissue, even after almost three months. He sank onto a chair, rolled up his pant leg and undid the brace that held the prosthesis in place. The relief was immediate. He reveled in it as he sat there, sipping his coffee. Unbidden, memories of the day he'd been injured filled his thoughts. To distract himself, he booted up his dad's laptop and checked his email.

A tap on the window drew Kyle's attention. Sara Kane stood watching him. He waited to see the revulsion his fiancée hadn't been able to hide. He searched for the disgust and loathing that had swum through her eyes when she'd seen his damaged limb. But Kyle couldn't find it in Sara's dark scrutiny and wondered why.

What could he do but wave her in? While she entered, he closed the computer and set it on his dad's desk.

"Good morning. I brought you some cinnamon buns." Her gaze moved from the computer to him. She closed the door behind her and set a pan on the table. Her gaze held his. "You didn't answer the doorbell."

"It's been broken since we moved in here. Dad was always going to fix it but—" Kyle realized he was rubbing his leg and quickly dragged his hand away. He was about to pull down his pant leg when she spoke.

"I could help you," she whispered. "If you want help."

"I don't." *Stop acting like a bear, Kyle.* "Thank you but I'll be fine, Sara." He didn't want her here, didn't want her to see his ugliness. "Don't worry about me."

Her solemn gaze locked with his but she said nothing.

"How did you get here?" He clenched his jaw against a leg cramp then gulped another mouthful of coffee, hoping that would help clear his fuzzy head.

"Laurel. She had to stop in town before picking up the boys from the airport. I wanted to ask you something so I told her I'd walk over here from the post office."

Kyle watched as Sara filled the kettle with water and switched it on. A moment later she'd found a basin under the sink and added a towel from the bathroom.

"What are you doing?" Kyle demanded through gritted teeth as waves of pain rolled in. He'd refused to take any pain reliever last night, knowing he had to learn to manage it or risk becoming addicted. And he couldn't afford that. He couldn't afford to become dependent on anyone or anything.

"Hot water will ease your soreness." Sara kept right on assembling things.

"Are you a nurse?" Kyle clamped his jaw together more tightly. Couldn't she see he wanted to be alone?

"If I say yes, will you let me help you?" she asked in a soft tone.

"No."

"I didn't think so." A flicker of a smile played with the corner of her lips but Sara kept right on working.

The woman had guts, Kyle admitted grudgingly as she added cold water to the basin, tossed in a handful of salt and set it on the floor in front of him. Because he craved relief, he didn't object when she poured boiling water from the kettle into the basin. Steam billowed up as she knelt in front of him. She dunked the towel, thoroughly soaked it then wrung it out. A moment later she wrapped the steaming towel around his stump and held it there, her hands gentle but confident.

Kyle almost groaned before he flinched away. No one outside the hospital staff had ever touched that ruined, angry part of him.

"Is it too hot?" She waggled her fingers in the water and frowned. "It doesn't feel too hot."

Actually it felt a lot like a warm hug.

"Kyle?"

He studied the top of her caramel-toned head. Somehow Sara's tender touch eased his yearning to be enveloped in his father's arms, something he'd craved during his intensive rehab and the weeks of therapy that followed.

"Kyle?" His name rushed from her lips, urgent. "Is it okay?" Her eyes were wide with—fear?

Why would she be afraid?

"It's fine," he groaned.

Liar. It is light years better than fine.

"I'm glad." A sweet smile lit up her entire face.

In the quietness of that moment Kyle couldn't help but compare Sara's response to the decimating reaction of the woman who'd claimed to love him. When she'd glimpsed his shattered limb in the veteran's hospital she had turned away and raced out, never to return.

Clearly, as he'd noticed several times, Sara was made of stronger stuff. His curiosity about her rose.

But Kyle didn't ask questions because the longer Sara's calm gaze held his, the more his muscles relaxed. She rinsed the cloth three times, each time reapplying and holding it in place until it cooled. Finally the knot of pain untied and slid away. He sighed his relief.

"The water's too cool now," Sara murmured. "I could heat more?"

"No. Thank you." Kyle felt half-bemused as he realized his whole body felt limp, as it had when he'd come out of the anesthetic after each of his surgeries. "Where did you learn to do that?" His curiosity about the strength in such a delicate-looking woman grew.

"My fos—brother used to get banged up. Hot salt-water cloths always helped him."

Sara's slight hesitation before she'd said *brother* and the way she stumbled over *banged up* intrigued Kyle. What story lay hidden beneath those few words?

"It's a great remedy." The way she'd knelt in front of him to care for him humbled Kyle. "Thank you," he said, and meant it.

"You're welcome." She rose in one fluid motion and glanced at the pan of rolls she'd left sitting on the table.

His father's favorite line from Milton's *Paradise Lost* flickered through Kyle's mind. "Grace was in all her steps, heaven in her eyes, in every gesture dignity and love." He'd never known anyone but his mom who'd so perfectly fit the description.

Until now.

"I'll just slip these buns into the oven to warm. You can rest for a while, then, when you're ready to eat, they'll be waiting." Sara tightened the foil around the container and placed it inside the oven.

It struck Kyle then that he was doing what he'd vowed not to. He was letting someone do things for him. He was letting himself become dependent.

"What did you want to ask me?" The question was perfunctory. He didn't want to hear. What he really wanted was for this disturbing woman to leave him alone.

Sara took her time dumping the basin, washing it out and storing it.

"Come on. I can't be that unapproachable," he prodded with a smile.

"Yes, you can." Sara looked straight at him, unsmiling. "But I'll ask anyway. I want to use something of yours."

"Use something—of mine?" That sounded as if she'd made it up on the spur of the moment. Maybe she was only here because she felt sorry for him. Kyle's gut burned. "Like what?"

"That." She pointed out the grimy window that overlooked his backyard.

Kyle followed her pointing finger. He couldn't figure out what she meant at first. There was nothing in the backyard. Except—

"I'd like permission to use your greenhouse, Kyle," she said.

"My mom's greenhouse." Past memories, very personal memories, of the joys he shared inside that greenhouse built inside his head but he suppressed them. Kyle was suddenly irrationally annoyed at the way Sara kept pushing her way into his world. All he wanted was to be alone. "What could you possibly want that for?"

"Last night Laurel told me some of the boys' histories so I'd understand why they're at Lives." She sat down. A tiny line furrowed her brow as she studied her hands. "I'm not sure I'm allowed to discuss them."

"I'll keep whatever you want to tell me confidential," Kyle promised, curiosity mounting.

"Laurel says one of the boys is quite withdrawn. Rod." She peeked through her lashes at him. "But he did very well when he was involved in a program at a tree nursery."

Kyle waited, surprised by her earnest tone.

"Of course, there aren't any tree nurseries here in Churchill," Sara said, "but I thought that if he could get involved in growing something, it might help. We don't have the capability at Lives. But I remembered seeing your greenhouse when we were here yesterday. If Rod could grow fresh herbs, I could use them in my cooking. Laurel said we'd share whatever we grew with you." Her silver-gray eyes never left his face. "If you agree to let us use the greenhouse, that is."

"I see." Kyle studied the glass structure. "The roof might not be stable, you know. I'd have to have it checked, maybe repaired."

A disappointed look flickered across her face. "You're saying no?"

"I'm saying I don't know." Kyle didn't want to reveal any sign of weakness, and having her see his injured leg made him feel weak, so he strapped on his prosthesis, rolled down his pant leg then slid his feet into a pair of his father's moccasins. "Let's go out and take a look."

"Okay." Sara pulled on the thin jacket she'd shed when she first came inside.

"You'll freeze if that's all you have to wear until summer gets here," he warned.

Sara chuckled, her smile brimming with something he couldn't quite define. All Kyle knew was that little seemed to faze this woman. A twinkle in those gorgeous eyes told him she'd faced much worse than cold weather, and come out on top.

"I'll be fine, Kyle."

He had a strong feeling that Sara Kane would be fine, though he couldn't have said why. Perhaps it was the resolute determination in her manner. Sara Kane wouldn't give up easily. He admired that.

"Open that cupboard. There should be a jacket in there, a red one." He didn't tell her the coat was special. He simply watched as she drew out his mother's red parka. "Try it on."

Sara shrugged into the coat. Her transformation was spectacular. A bird of paradise—she looked magnificent, delicate and incongruous in this land of icy winds and frozen tundra. The color lent life to her, enhancing subtle undertones in her hair and making her skin glow with a beauty Kyle had almost missed.

"I don't think any of our guests ever looked as good as you in that."

"Your guests?" She pulled the faux-fur collar around her ears and studied herself in the mirror, seemingly bemused by what she saw.

"Dad and I ran a guiding company," he told her. "There are gloves in the pockets, I think."

"Guiding? What does that mean?" She pulled on the gloves and bent her fingers experimentally, as if she expected the gloves' thickness to impede movement.

"Guiding tourists to see the local sights," he explained. "The northern lights, whale watching in a Zodiac, ATV treks into the wilderness or jaunts to see the polar bears—we did it all." Bitterness oozed between his words, rendering his tone brittle and harsh, but even though he heard it, Kyle found it impossible to suppress his sense of utter loss.

"Polar bears." Sara's eyes were huge. She peeked over her shoulder as if expecting one to pounce from the bedroom.

"Churchill is famous for its polar bears. But it's late in the season. When the ice goes out they leave to hunt seals. This year it's very early but the ice is almost gone. Global warming, I suppose." Kyle hated the fear pinching her pretty face. He rushed to reassure her. "But even if some bears are still hanging around, you don't have to worry. There's a town patrol that does a good job of keeping tabs on the bears' whereabouts. Sometimes you'll hear gunshots—pops," he modified when her eyes expanded even more. "The noises deter the bears. I didn't hear any on the way here yesterday or so far this morning, so it should be okay."

"Uh-huh." Sara inhaled and thrust back her shoulders as if she were about to venture into battle.

"Listen, Sara." Kyle leaned forward. "Before we go outside I want to tell you something."

"Okay." It looked like she was holding her breath.

"Churchill is very safe." He grabbed his jacket off the hook near the door. "But we tell this to everyone who comes here to prepare them. Just in case."

"In case." She gulped. "Right."

"It might seem counterintuitive to you, but if you do happen upon a bear, do not turn your back on him and do not run." *Gently. Don't terrorize her, Kyle.* "Either of those actions will make you look like prey to him."

"Which I will be," she pointed out in a whisper, her face now devoid of all color.

"Well, yes." He had to smile. "But what you want is to look like his adversary. Make yourself as tall as possible. Put your arms in the air and wave them. Yell as loud as you can. But do not run." Why did he suddenly feel he had to protect her? "Bears love the chase."

"Okay." She trembled, her alarm visible.

Kyle had wanted Sara to be cautious. Instead he'd alarmed her.

Her eyes lost their silver sheen and darkened. She looked petrified.

Way to go, Kyle.

"I'd offer to drive you back, but I don't think I could drive, even if Dad's old truck was running. He cracked it up just before—" He swallowed, forced himself to continue. "Anyway, I don't have transport."

"I'm sure I'll be fine." Sara didn't look fine. She looked like someone who had dredged up her last ounce of courage to face the lion's den.

"Yes, you will be," Kyle agreed. "Now let's go take a look at Mom's greenhouse." He rose, ignored the twinge of pain in his hip and followed her outside, embarrassed by his slow progress down the stairs and Sara's obvious attempt to ignore it.

Kyle didn't intend to be in Churchill long, but by the time he reached the bottom step he'd made up his mind to hire someone to build a ramp. Dragging himself up and down these stairs sucked the energy out of him, not to mention that it made him feel like some kind of spectacle.

"Okay?" Sara opened the gate to his backyard.

"Just dandy." He chose his steps over the uneven ground carefully. What a fool he'd been to wear these soft leather slippers and risk injuring himself again.

"The structure looks good," Sara said, her head tilted to one side like a curious bird as she peered at the glass roof. "Of course, I don't really know anything about greenhouses."

"A friend wrote that he'd check on things till I could get home. It looks like he's made sure everything is still solid." Kyle pressed against the metal frame. Nothing swayed. "I brought the key. Let me check inside."

The door swung to with a loud creak. Inside, the glass was dingy with years of dust. Debris covered parts of the floor.

"Oh, my." Sara stared like a deer caught in headlights.

"After Mom passed away, Dad and I never used this for anything much but storage. I should have cleaned it out." Kyle pulled away the cobwebs. "It's filthy."

"It won't take long to clean." Obviously recovered, Sara pressed the toe of her shoe against a stack of plastic bins. "What are these?"

"I don't know. Dad must have packed them." Kyle turned a pail upside down and sat on it. Then he opened the top bin. A bundle of bubble wrap lay inside. He lifted it out and slowly unwrapped it. A notebook fell out.

Instantly Kyle was a kid again, rushing home from school to find his mom in here, scribbling in her gardening journal while Dad teased her about her addiction to roses. Kyle gasped at the overwhelming pain.

"Kyle, what's wrong?" Sara hunkered down in front of him. Her hand covered his. "Are you in pain?" she asked ever so gently.

"Yes." For once he wasn't ashamed to admit it. His heart ached so deeply he felt as if life had drained out of his body. He fought to be free, but the ache blemished his spirit like a scab on a scar.

"Can I help?"

"I'm okay." Kyle inhaled, forced away the sadness. "This is my mom's journal. I didn't realize we still had it." He flipped through the pages, chuckling at the funny drawings his mom had made. "She was always trying to produce a new breed of rose."

"Under these conditions?" Sara lifted one eyebrow in surprise.

"Yes. Look." He held up the book to show the sketch. "This was going to be her Oliver rose—named in memory of her high school friend. But the Oliver rose couldn't take Churchill's harshness. He was too weak."

He was suddenly aware of Sara, crouched behind him, peering over his shoulder.

"I can't read her writing."

"No one could." He cleared his throat. "Listen. 'My dear Oliver is a wuss. One chilly night without the heater and he's lost all his leaves. Pfui! A weakling. And a reminder of what God expects of us, a stiff backbone that weathers life's challenges. I want a rose that will use the negatives of life to get tough and still bloom. I'll wait and try again next year. But I fear my Oliver rose is finished.'" Kyle smiled. "She always spoke of her roses as if they were people."

"It sounds like she had a sense of humor," Sara said.

"A wicked one. Listen to this." Kyle read her another passage about a yellow rosebush a friend had sent them. His laughter joined Sara's. "I remember that bush. Coral Bells. It lasted year after year, no matter what adversity it encountered. My mother put Oliver next to it to give him some gumption. But it didn't help." He closed the book, suddenly loath to continue revealing these precious memories. "I wonder what else is in this box."

To hide his emotions, Kyle tugged out layers of old newspaper, aware that Sara still crouched beside him, neatly folding each piece of paper he tossed on the ground. Below the paper lay trophies from school sports, local awards he and his father had won for their business, a book filled with clippings and letters from past customers—he kept pulling them out until finally the box was empty.

"Garbage." Kyle refused to be swamped by memories again while Sara watched. "I should chuck them." He set aside the plastic box and began working on the second bin. But it, too, was filled with childhood mementos that only served to remind him of things he could no longer do.

At the very bottom lay a series of Sunday-school

awards and a big ribbon with *top place* printed on it in silver letters, from the championship quiz team he'd once led.

"More garbage." Bitterness surged that God hadn't been there when Kyle had needed Him, despite his faith and despite the many pleas he'd sent heavenward. "No need to keep any of this."

But Sara was already rewrapping each item and laying it carefully back into the container.

"Looks like this is the last one Dad got around to packing." Kyle paused, needing breathing space so he could face whatever came next without revealing to Sara how affected he was. "My father the pack rat must have needed room in the house."

"I think he wanted to keep your special things safe for you," Sara said, her voice firm yet soft. "So you wouldn't forget your history."

"Maybe." He yanked off the last lid and tossed away the flat sheet of plain brown paper lying on top.

And stared at the contents.

Sara's fingers curved around his shoulder.

He felt stupid, awkward and juvenile. But he could do nothing to stop the tears. They rolled down his hot cheeks and landed on his wrinkled shirt in a trickle that quickly became a river.

Kyle lifted out the familiar wooden box, letting the satin smoothness of the wood soak through to his hands, waiting for it to thaw his heart.

"Kyle?" Sara's gentle voice bloomed with anxiety. But she said no more, waiting patiently until he finally pulled his emotions under control. "What is it?"

"A seed box," he told her. His index finger traced the letters he'd carved on the lid years earlier. "It was a Christmas gift Dad helped me make for my mom when I was twelve." He lifted open the top, slid out one of the drawers, brushed a fingertip against the velvet lining inside.

"It's beautiful." Sara leaned forward to examine the surface. "Is it rosewood?"

"Yes," he said, surprised by her knowledge. "I had to order the wood specially. I thought we'd never get it done in time." The laugh burst from him, harsh and painful. "Actually, I guess we didn't."

"What do you mean?" Sara sounded slightly breathless.

"Mom had barely put her seeds in this when she was diagnosed with breast cancer. By planting time she was too sick to come out here anymore." He snapped the lid closed and thrust the box inside the bin. "She was so sure God would heal her. She said over and over, 'Trust in God, Kyle. He'll never let you down.'" Fury burned inside, a white-hot rage that could not be doused. "Well, He did. He let me down twice. And I will never trust Him again."

He rose and made his way to the door, not caring about his awkwardness. All he wanted was to get away, to hide out until he found a way to deal with his anger.

"Do whatever you want in here, Sara. You're welcome to it. Just don't ask me to help you." With that, Kyle stepped outside. He stood there, eyes closed as he inhaled the fresh, crisp air into his lungs and blew out frustration.

You're starting over, he reminded himself. *Forget the past.*

Behind him he heard Sara close the greenhouse door with a quiet click. Desperate to be alone, he headed for the stairs to the house. He almost cheered when behind him a horn tooted and broke the strained silence. Kyle glanced over one shoulder at Sara.

"It's Laurel," she said. One hand went to the zipper of the red coat.

"Keep it. You might need it." He held her gaze, nodding when her eyes asked him if he was sure.

"Thank you." She hesitated then lifted her chin. "And thank you for letting us use the greenhouse. Enjoy your cinnamon buns."

"Thanks." He watched her walk to Laurel's van. She opened the door then turned to face him.

"God bless you, Kyle," she said in the softest voice. "I'll stop by tomorrow."

"That's not necess—" Kyle's words fell on emptiness. Sara was gone, the van driving away.

Kyle stomped into the house, fuming. He didn't

want her here, checking on him, blessing him. He wanted to be alone, to become totally self-sufficient.

Yet as he sampled the sticky sweetness of the cinnamon buns, Kyle almost welcomed the thought of someone else, someone whose presence would stop him from being engulfed by bitterness at what he'd lost.

He stopped himself. His plan for the future did not include staying here or becoming dependent. It certainly could not include getting mesmerized by a pair of silvery-gray eyes. He would never allow himself to be that vulnerable again.

For now, Kyle was home. He'd take the rest of his life one step at a time.

But if Sara did come back, he'd try to find out more about her, like what had made her stare so longingly at his dad's laptop when she'd seen it lying on the desk.

And why she seemed so certain God would bless him.

Chapter Four

"Have a wonderful day, Rod," Sara said as the tall, quiet boy shuffled his backpack over his shoulders, the last of the six boys to leave. "Enjoy your first day of school. And don't forget we're going to the greenhouse this afternoon."

Rod nodded, staring at her for several minutes. "You're sure it's okay?"

"Pretty sure." She patted his shoulder at the sound of Laurel tooting the van's horn. "You'd better go."

He gave her another of those silent, soulful looks before he left.

"Arriving near the end of the year like this can't be easy for him, for any of them," she mused aloud. "But surely they'll be okay, won't they, Lord? Laurel said the school agreed to hold summer courses to get them up to speed and ready for a new term in the fall. Please help them all use this opportunity."

Feeling a bit self-conscious about talking aloud,

Sara refocused, wrinkling her nose at the stack of dishes.

"What a mess. I think I'll leave cleanup until after I finish prepping for dinner." Humming to herself, Sara retrieved a box of apples from the storeroom then realized there wasn't enough counter space.

"Okay, then. Cleaning it is." As she got to work washing and scrubbing away the remains of breakfast, she sang a praise chorus she'd learned at the church she'd attended in Vancouver. She'd barely made a dent in the mess when a small, delicate hand covered hers.

"Oh!" She jerked away in surprise.

"I'm sorry. I didn't mean to startle you." The very proper English voice came from a tiny woman dressed in trim jeans and a fitted white blouse. Her silver hair had been caught in a knot on the top of her head, revealing periwinkle-blue eyes that sparkled like stars when she smiled. "I'm Lucy Clow. And this is my husband, Hector."

"It's very nice to meet you." Sara blinked. "I'm afraid Laurel is—"

"On her way to school with the boys." Lucy nodded. "She knew we were coming." She lifted the scraper from Sara's fingers. "Let me do this. Hector and I are here to help." The loving glance she gave the tall, bald man made Sara wish someone would look at her like that.

"I do have a few things planned for today," Sara

admitted. *Including cleaning Kyle's greenhouse this afternoon*. Having met Rod, she was confident he would enjoy working there. "Would you like a cup of coffee before you start?"

When Hector cleared his throat, Lucy chuckled. "Hector's hinting that he needs a good cup of coffee before he starts work on Laurel's computer room."

Computer room? Laurel hadn't mentioned setting up a computer room.

The thought of it brought Sara a burst of anticipation. But she reminded herself that having a computer and being able to use one were two different things.

She'd wanted so badly to ask Kyle about teaching her when she'd been to his house the other morning. His computer had been sitting right there, but she'd hesitated because he'd been in such pain when she arrived. Besides, wasn't asking for use of the greenhouse enough for one day?

"I've just made a fresh pot." She poured two cups. "I thought Laurel would need it when she returns."

"I can imagine." Lucy laughed. "Those poor boys are probably nervous about their first day." She sipped her coffee then set it down and got to work, her hands moving with lightning-quick speed as she rinsed and stacked plates.

Hector, too, seemed in a rush as he quickly drank his coffee.

"Please relax and enjoy your coffee, both of you.

And, Lucy, it's very kind of you to help me while Hector's working, but don't feel you must. This is my job."

"Laurel says you're very good at it, too." The blue eyes twinkled. "I am *not* good at cooking, as Hector will tell you. But I'm very good at cleaning." Lucy stacked the dishwasher deftly. Sara had never used one before and she hadn't quite mastered loading it properly. "I like cleaning, don't you?"

"Not so much." Sara began washing the apples. "I won't refuse your help because I want to get going on these apples for pies."

"Those boys will love homemade apple pie, won't they, Hector?" Lucy's husband nodded but said nothing.

"You live in Churchill?" Sara began paring the apples.

"We do now." Lucy turned on the dishwasher then picked up a knife and joined Sara. "We used to be missionaries to the Inuit in a community much farther north than Churchill. We're retired from that now, but we believe God can still use us." She winked at Hector. "Since we don't have children, folks in Churchill are our family. So that makes you our family, too—Sara, isn't it?"

"I should have introduced myself. Yes, I'm Sara Kane." She was dumbfounded by the enthusiastic welcome these strangers offered. "It's nice to meet you."

"You, too. This project is so worthwhile," Lucy said in a more serious tone. "Each of us is under construction throughout our lives as God works on us, but it's doubly true for these young boys. What an appropriate name Laurel chose."

"Yes." Sara frowned. She hadn't thought about her life as being under construction but Lucy was right. It was.

"Why don't I finish peeling these apples while you start your pastry?"

Hector interrupted to thank Sara for the coffee then disappeared. Apparently he'd already received his instructions about Laurel's computer room. Lucy continued to work, humming while her knife whizzed over the apples.

After lining five pie plates, Sara had a small amount of pastry dough left. An idea occurred. After searching the cupboards, she finally found an individual-size foil dish and spread dough in that, too.

"Making a pie for someone special?" Lucy asked in a coy voice.

"Oh. No." Sara blushed. As if she'd have someone special in her life. "It's— I thought I'd make one for Kyle Loness. He's just arrived home and—"

"Yes, we heard. So sad that his father wasn't here to see him." Lucy closed her eyes. Her lips moved but no sound was audible. When she opened her eyes and found Sara watching her, she smiled. "I like to remind God of His needy kids."

Besides Laurel, Sara had never met anyone so open about their faith.

"Hector and I organized a cleanup of Kyle's yard last week but we didn't touch the greenhouse. We intend to stop by on our way home and ask him if we can help with that, too." Lucy finished paring the apples then asked if she could prepare vegetables for dinner.

"I thought we'd have carrots for dinner."

"Great." Lucy looked delighted by the chore. "I'm sure Kyle will love your thoughtfulness," she said. "As I recall, his mom's pie was always first to go at the church socials."

After yesterday, the last thing Sara wanted to do was revive more of Kyle's memories of his mother. Too late now, she ignored her hesitation and listened to Lucy describe her life as a missionary as she finished. Then she slid all the pies into the big, old-fashioned baker's oven. But she hesitated only a moment before she set the smallest pie inside the oven. If Kyle didn't want it, someone else would.

Sara's thoughts wandered to the handsome veteran. How was Kyle this morning? Was his leg still hurting him? The part inside of her hadn't felt like a misfit when she'd tried to ease his pain. She'd felt useful, as if he needed her.

"Sara?"

She suddenly realized Lucy had asked her something. "Sorry?"

"I was just being nosy, wondering how you'd met Kyle." Lucy winked.

"We arrived in Churchill on the same train," Sara explained as she bagged the rest of the apple slices and packed them into the freezer. A quick cleanup then she assembled the ingredients for peanut butter cookies. Laurel had told her people would often drop in and that Sara should be prepared to offer a snack or even a meal at a moment's notice. Time to start building a larder reserve.

"Kyle was always such a gentleman," Lucy mused. "He's the kind of man who isn't afraid to open a door or lend you an arm if the ground is rough. A real hero type. I don't know why more young men don't understand how attractive that is."

"Kyle is nice," Sara murmured, her cheeks burning under Lucy's scrutiny. "He's agreed to let me use his mother's greenhouse for a project with one of the boys."

Lucy's eyes widened. "Kyle hasn't allowed anyone to touch that greenhouse since his mom's death—"

Lucy was interrupted by noises from the front hall.

Laurel's laughter echoed to them, followed by a rumbled response lower than Hector's voice. To Sara it sounded like Kyle. Immediately her pulse began to flutter. Had he come to take back his offer about the greenhouse? Laurel bounded into the room. When she saw Lucy she wrapped the tiny woman in a hug.

"Bless you and Hector for coming so quickly. I appreciate it." She turned to Sara. "You met Lucy, right? Isn't she a wonder?"

"Yes, she is," Sara agreed with a smile for the vibrant senior. "I've appreciated her help."

"I knew you would." Laurel waited as Lucy excused herself to answer her cell phone in another room then said, "Kyle's taking off his coat. He agreed to look at my computer to see if he can get rid of the gremlin that's taken over."

"That's nice," Sara said, hearing the breathlessness in her voice. It was nice that Kyle was here. *Nice?* Sara scoffed at herself. She was getting good at understatement.

He walked into the kitchen.

"Good morning, Kyle." Sara pretended her stomach hadn't turned into a jellied mush.

"Hi." His response emerged in a low growl. A tic at the corner of his mouth told her he was hurting and wanted to sit.

Sara pretended she needed to check the oven so she could move closer to him. "Are you okay?" she whispered.

"For now." His smile seemed a little forced.

"I haven't told him yet, Sara," Laurel said, her grin stretched across her face, "but I'm hoping that by the time Kyle gets the kinks out of my laptop, I'll have persuaded him to get some of those old desktop computers running for the boys."

"I suspected you wanted more when you asked me about my dad's stock of parts," Kyle said, his smile wry. "Marla didn't tell me you were so devious."

"That's because she doesn't know. Yet." Laurel chuckled then sniffed. "Something smells very good, Sara. How long before whatever's in that oven is ready to eat?"

"I'm baking apple pies. They won't be finished for a while." A flutter of nervousness wrapped around Sara's stomach as she met Kyle's gaze. A new thought occurred to her. Maybe he felt she'd been too forward when she applied the hot cloths to his leg. Did he think she'd been too presumptuous? And why did it matter so much? "There's fresh banana loaf. I made it before breakfast for the boys' lunches."

"Perfect. But we're not having coffee yet. Kyle has to earn his snack first." Laurel linked her arm in Kyle's so he had to leave the room with her.

"What a taskmaster you work for, Sara," he complained as he left.

Sara was still chuckling when Lucy returned and asked what was so funny.

"You see, such a gentleman," Lucy said after Sara's explanation. She nodded her silver head. "He didn't even refuse her."

"I don't know many people who can refuse Laurel." Sara slid a sheet of her cookies in the second oven. Then she set a large pot on the stove, adding a chicken and some of the vegetables Lucy had prepared.

"What's that for?" Lucy asked.

"Soup for lunch. You will be staying, won't you?"

"We'd love to," Lucy replied promptly. "In fact, I just reminded God that Hector will want lunch in a couple of hours and I have nothing at home."

Sara couldn't help laughing. When had she last felt so lighthearted? *Lucy feels like family, God— but I still want my own.*

By the time the cookies were cooling, her side ached from laughing at Lucy's stories. Then Kyle appeared in the doorway and Sara's breath snagged in her throat. She was glad his attention was focused elsewhere.

"Good morning, Mrs. Clow." His tone was grave, solemn.

"For goodness' sake, Kyle." The diminutive woman rushed up to him and wrapped her arms around his waist. "After all these years can't I finally be plain old Lucy?"

"I don't think you could ever be plain old anything," Kyle murmured, a hint of tenderness softening his usually harsh tone.

"I'm so glad you're home safe and sound, my dear boy." Lucy's voice brimmed with emotion. "So glad. Hector and I prayed for you every day."

"Thanks." As Kyle awkwardly patted her back, his eyes met Sara's. He was obviously uncomfortable with Lucy's effusive hug but he made no effort to shift away.

Sara loved that though Kyle was not a "toucher," he tolerated Lucy's embrace without complaint, even gently hugging her back before Lucy finally drew away.

Lucy was right. Kyle was exactly what most women would want in a man.

"Before she got caught on the phone, Laurel said I'm to tell you we need coffee," he said to Sara.

Sara studied Kyle for a moment, noting the way he rubbed his temple. He looked tired.

"She insists those computer relics she tore apart can be reassembled into working computers." He rolled his eyes. "She must think I'm a magician."

"Laurel does have a way of coaxing more from you," Lucy agreed. "But since it's to help these precious boys, I can't complain."

"I shouldn't, either," Kyle mumbled. "Lives Under Construction is an excellent project. It's just—"

His gaze met Sara's and she immediately understood that he'd planned to do other things today. "I guess I'll have to learn to be flexible," he said with a shrug.

"With Laurel we all have to learn that," she agreed.

The corners of his lips tipped up in the tiniest smile, but it made a world of difference to Sara. Suddenly the day seemed much brighter. But why? Kyle should be nothing to her, just a means to the greenhouse, that was all. And yet, because he smiled at her, her heart beat more rapidly. To hide her reaction she took out the banana loaf and began slicing it.

"Something smells wonderful." Kyle's face tilted up, his nose in the air.

"Apple pie, just like your mom's." Lucy beamed. "Sara even made you your own special one. Isn't that sweet?"

Sara gulped, embarrassed that she'd drawn attention to the fact.

"It's very kind of you to think of me, Sara," Kyle said after a pause.

"It's nothing. I'm trying to use up some old apples is all," Sara rushed to explain. "I didn't know you were coming here today. I thought I'd drop it off when Rod and I go to the greenhouse this afternoon."

"About that—"

"I've explained it to him," she said, desperate to prevent Kyle from telling her he'd changed his mind. "He's eager to get started with our plan. After school we'll clean all that glass."

"Uh-huh." Kyle glanced at Lucy as if he wanted to say something.

"I didn't know you were thinking of allowing people to use the greenhouse, Kyle." The blue in Lucy's gaze intensified.

"I wasn't," he admitted. "But as you said, if it's to help this Lives project, we shouldn't complain."

Sara smothered a laugh at the way Kyle had deflected Lucy's comment, but she doubted the former missionary would be silenced so easily. She gulped when his attention turned to her.

"As I told you, Sara, no one's been in the greenhouse for a while," Kyle reminded. "Hector's agreed to check it out after lunch. You and Rod will have to wait until he gives the okay."

"That will be fine." His slight smile and the way his gaze held hers for an infinitesimal moment sent a tingle straight to that needy spot inside Sara. Thankfully the timer beeped. She broke the electric connection that seemed to hum between them by turning away to mix up some biscuit dough to go with her soup. What on earth was wrong with her?

Laurel and Hector arrived and took their place at the table.

"I love how your baking smells fill the whole place." Laurel accepted her coffee with a grin. "It gives Lives exactly the homey atmosphere I want for the boys."

Embarrassed by her praise, Sara busied herself filling cups. By then the only seat left at the table was beside Kyle.

She did not want to sit there.

She wasn't sure why except that being around him

somehow made her feel awkward, as if she had an upset stomach or was off balance.

Feeling out of place, Sara checked on her pies then began cleaning the mixing bowl and utensils she'd used.

"Sara, come and join us. You deserve a break." Lucy's smile made her blue eyes look guileless. "There's a space for you beside Kyle."

Sara tried to refuse, but it was easier just to sit down beside Kyle. She was far too aware of him sitting next to her, shifting frequently just like her.

It came as a relief when everyone finally finished and rose to leave. But Sara jumped up too quickly and bumped against Kyle.

"I'm sorry," she exclaimed, cheeks burning when he grasped the table edge to balance himself. "I'm so clumsy."

"It wasn't you. It was me," he said, wincing. "I haven't quite got the hang of this new leg they gave me. My therapist insists I checked myself out of therapy too early, so it's my own fault."

"Can I help?" she offered, shy but unwilling to let him hurt if she could somehow assuage it. Besides, everyone had gone. If he refused her help, no one would see her embarrassment at being rejected.

"How? More hot salt cloths?" he teased.

"If they'll help, yes," she said steadily, meeting his gaze head-on, though her face grew warm under his stare.

Kyle looked at her for so long that she began to wish she hadn't made the offer.

"Never mind. I should—"

He cut her off. "I don't think I've ever known anyone like you, Sara Kane."

"Is that a good thing or a bad thing?" she whispered.

Kyle chuckled. It was the first time she'd heard true mirth in his voice.

"Time will tell, Sara." With that he left for the computer room, his gait odd and uneven but determined.

Sara had no idea what he'd meant.

"Are those pies in danger of burning?" Lucy asked from the doorway, breaking into her reverie. Sara hurried to open the oven as Lucy flipped her phone closed. "I think Kyle likes you," she said.

"I hope so. I could use a friend." Sara turned away to concentrate on her work but inside a bubble of happiness rose. She hoped Kyle liked her, she hoped it with every fiber of her being, because she was beginning to like him a lot. Friendship was okay, wasn't it?

Friendship with a man? In a flood of uncertainty her feelings took a tumble. She wasn't good at relationships. She certainly didn't know how to be friends with a man like Kyle. He was an acquaintance but that was all he was. That was all he could be, because she didn't have anything to offer him, even if she was interested.

Sighing, she lifted out each golden sizzling pie and set it on a cooling rack.

"Now what can I do?" Lucy asked.

"You've already done so much."

"I don't mean with kitchen work." Lucy's hands rested on her shoulders. Gently she eased Sara around to face her. "Tell me what's troubling you."

"What you said about Kyle—him liking me, I mean." Sara gulped. "I don't know what to do about it. I've never had a man as a friend before. It scares me. Maybe I'll do something stupid to offend him. Or maybe, when he gets to know me, he'll regret it. I haven't been anywhere or done anything important, like him. All I can do is cook."

Shame suffused her. How dorky she sounded, like a stupid, dumb kid.

"And you cook extremely well, Sara." Lucy brushed a hand over her hair. "But why would you think Kyle would reject friendship with you? Has he done or said something—"

"No, not at all," Sara interrupted, ashamed that she had somehow made Lucy think ill of Kyle. "It's just—I've been praying God would give me some friends. I've never had any, you see. I just didn't think someone like Kyle would want to be my friend." Lucy seemed to understand.

"I think you're going to find a lot of friends in

Churchill, my dear. I would be honored to be your first." She held out her hand.

"Thank you," Sara said as she folded Lucy's hand in hers, thrilled that this woman thought of her as a friend.

Could You help Kyle think of me like that, too, God?

"Isn't there something you'd rather do than watch me fiddle with this mess?"

Kyle glared at Sara, wondering why she hung around when it was clear this computer was not going to function properly without a major overhaul.

"I want to learn about computers," Sara said.

He raised his eyebrows at her.

"I don't know anything about them." She bit her bottom lip, something he now recognized as a habit she employed when embarrassed. "It sounds stupid for somebody my age, but I don't even know how to operate one. Where I grew up, we didn't have computers."

"Oh." He cursed his insensitivity.

"I'm hoping you get one of these running soon so Rod can show me how to use it." Sara lowered her lids, hiding the expression in her eyes.

"Rod?" Kyle soldered two wires together and tested the connection. "Isn't he the boy you want to work with in the greenhouse?"

"Yes. Apparently he's very good on computers.

He plans to set up a web page in memory of his uncle." Sara frowned, her silvery eyes darkening. "That is what it's called, right? A web page?"

"Uh-huh." Kyle held his breath and pressed the on switch. He clenched his fist at the popping sound as sparks sprayed across his workbench. "Piece of junk." He smacked his fist in the center of the circuit board. "This is hopeless."

"You can't make it work?" Sara's face fell as if she'd lost her best friend.

"I'm good but I'm no magician." Kyle wished he didn't feel responsible for those gray clouds in her eyes. "There's a reason people get rid of old computers, you know." He rubbed his eyes with one hand and the knot in his shoulder with the other. Then he glanced at his watch. "I'd better get home. I can't do any more today."

"You've been at this a long time," Sara agreed.

Kyle looked up, and found he couldn't make himself look away from her. The sun poured in the window, amplifying her simple beauty, holding him spellbound. When she smiled his breath caught in his throat—until he realized her smile was directed at someone else.

"Come in, Rod," she said. "I want you to meet Kyle. He owns the greenhouse. He's also trying to fix these computers for you."

"Hey." Rod nodded at Kyle, glanced at the array spread over the workbench and shook his head. The thirteen-year-old made a face. "Wasting your time. They're pieces of junk."

Kyle let out a shout of laughter. "I agree with you wholeheartedly, buddy."

"So?" Rod stared at him.

"There's nothing here worth salvaging." Kyle shifted under those intensely dark eyes.

"Uh-huh." Life seemed to drain out of Rod.

"Sara said you're planning to set up a web page. About what?"

Kyle wasn't sure why he was asking. He had his own life to figure out. But there was something about this kid that gnawed at him. He seemed so totally deflated over the loss of the computers.

"It's uh, personal. You know?" Rod shrugged.

"Yeah, I know about personal." Kyle hated showing his disability in public but his leg was bothering him something fierce. He'd been seated for too long. He tried to rise, grabbed the side of the bench for balance and forced himself upright, grateful when Sara's hand supported him.

"Kyle was injured in Afghanistan," Sara explained.

Kyle's anger bubbled up. He wondered why she'd said that. He glared at her but she was watching Rod so he did, too, and was stunned by the grief that covered the boy's face. A long silence ensued.

"My uncle died there." Rod stared at the floor. After a moment, he lifted his head and glanced at Sara. At her nod he continued. "He was like a father to me. I want to create a web page in his memory, so other soldiers can check in and remember their friends who died," he said.

Stunned by the boy's selflessness, Kyle glanced at Sara. Her silver eyes sparkled with unshed tears.

"I don't want to forget him," Rod murmured. "Nobody should forget the people who died so we can be free." His hands clenched at his sides. "A guy at school said the best thing would be to forget my uncle, the war and everything. He said we should get on with life and that my uncle was a loser. One day I couldn't take it anymore so I beat him up."

Kyle's gut tied in a knot. He was suddenly aware that his hands were fisted and that every muscle in his body had tensed. Anger gripped him. Suddenly, helping Rod set up his web page was very important.

"We'll get a computer running for you, Rod," he said. "Don't worry."

"Thanks." The boy's sadness seemed to melt away. "Some of the other guys need it to stay in contact with their families. Letters aren't as good as email."

"I hear you," Kyle said, remembering the many emails he'd shared with his dad. He lifted his head, and caught Sara studying him with that beautiful smile and his heart did something funny. "I am going to make sure Lives Under Construction gets a computer lab," he assured her before he could stop himself.

"I believe you will, Kyle," she said with complete faith. "I trust you."

I believe you will, Kyle.

I trust you.

Was it possible that she truly meant those things? Could she believe in him and trust him?

Kyle was astonished by what those simple words did to him. And in that moment, he resolved not to let down sweet Sara Kane.

Chapter Five

"Thanks for helping me, Teddy." Kyle couldn't stifle his grin as his father's best friend carried the last carton from the train station and set it inside the truck bed.

"Absolutely my pleasure." Teddy Stonechild slammed the truck gate closed. "Do we need to stop somewhere else?"

"Nope. We'll go straight to Lives," Kyle told him. A heady delight filled him as he imagined how Sara would react to his surprise.

"Uh, listen, Kyle." Teddy sat in the truck, waiting for him to fasten his seat belt, a troubled look on his face. "It might not be the best idea for me to go along with you."

"What do you mean?" Kyle frowned at him. "You've only been back in Churchill a day. You haven't seen what Lives Under Construction is like now that the boys are here."

"True. But when I was here before I, well, I kind of made an enemy of Laurel Quinn." Teddy shrugged. "It wasn't intentional and I'd take it back if I could, but that isn't going to happen."

Kyle frowned. Teddy liked everyone. "How did you make an enemy of Laurel?"

"I mentioned my, uh, concerns about her project to the town council earlier this year." Teddy looked sheepish as he explained. "Well," he said defensively, "you know how often I've stayed here. I feel like part of the community and that's how they treat me. So I told the truth."

"You dissed her project? Publicly?" Kyle winced.

"That's not all." Teddy's face turned bright red.

"What else?" Kyle asked cautiously.

"I guess I came on a little too strong with my objections. She had to, well, jump through some extra hoops before they granted approval." Teddy looked totally abashed.

"That's not like you." Kyle frowned. "You usually welcome everyone who comes to town."

"And I tried to welcome her. But something about Laurel Quinn and her plan got under my skin," Teddy admitted. "She doesn't seem like a good business manager," he defended.

"Given the job she's trying to do, I'm not sure the business part matters as much as helping those kids. She's not the CEO of your hotel chain, you know." Kyle shrugged. "Anyway, that's in the past.

Just promise me that today you'll keep your issues to yourself," he said.

"Of course." Teddy looked offended. "It's a moot point now, anyway. The place is up and running."

"And doing good work," Kyle added.

"So you've said." Teddy gave him an odd sideways look. "I heard you're letting the cook use your mom's greenhouse." Teddy had always had a soft spot for Kyle's mother.

"Her name is Sara and yes, I have agreed. She's using it to help a kid named Rod. They're going to grow herbs or something."

"Sara, huh?"

"Sara Kane." Kyle's face burned at Teddy's narrowed scrutiny. Funny how his heartbeat accelerated just saying her name. "I decided to let them use it until I sell the place and move on."

"You're still determined to do that?" Teddy asked.

"Yes. There's nothing for me here now. I can't do the things I did and I won't become dependent on others." The grimness of his future sucked away Kyle's joy. "You know what my injuries mean. I can never have kids, never be a father. It's too hard to be here and know that. I'll leave and find something else."

"Doing what?" Teddy frowned at him.

"I haven't quite figured that out yet." Kyle clamped his mouth shut until they drove into the yard site. He did not want to think about leaving Churchill right now.

"Kyle, hello." Sara met them at the door, wearing his mother's red jacket. His heart gave a thunk but it wasn't sadness, more like appreciation. She looked good.

"Leaving?" he asked.

"I was going to do some more work on the greenhouse," she said. "Lucy and Hector brought us some used bikes, so I can ride to your place now. It won't take as long." She smiled at Teddy. "Hello. I'm Sara."

Kyle introduced them.

"Nice to meet you," Teddy said in his usual affable tone. "Is Laurel here?"

"She's out, I'm afraid." Sara watched him unload three boxes from his truck. "Is that a delivery for her?"

"Sort of." Kyle held the door open for Teddy. "It's this way," he said, walking toward the computer room. "If you'll bring in the rest, I'll begin unpacking."

"Sure." Teddy left for another load.

"What is all this, Kyle?" Sara watched as he slid his box knife under the tape and ripped open the box. He felt her freeze when she read the side of the box. "Are those—?"

"Computers." He grinned as he lifted out a tower. "Six of the latest models. All Teddy and I have to do is get them operational and you guys are set."

"Six computers? But how did you get them?" Sara's silver-gray eyes stretched wide.

"I ordered them a couple of days ago. They arrived on the train this morning." He didn't understand her hesitation or the worried look she gave him.

"But Laurel says we're on a very tight budget." She bit her bottom lip. "I'm sure she can't afford—"

"Don't worry," he said, anxious to ease her obvious distress. "These are paid for."

"How? Laurel never mentioned—"

"I paid for them. Or rather, Dad did. He left some money he said should be used for a good cause. I think this is a good cause and I know he'd agree." He winked at her, wanting to share the joy that bubbled inside at being able to give. "Plus it will save me spending more frustrating hours on those relics of Laurel's."

Sara simply stared at him, as if she didn't believe he was serious.

"Can you hold this box so I can slide out the tower?" Kyle waited for her to shrug out of the red jacket, then with her help, lifted out the monitors and towers. Teddy arranged the units on the tables Hector had built, and then carried out the empty boxes.

Eager to get everything up and running, Kyle began connecting the systems, only too aware of Sara's intense scrutiny over his shoulder.

"Can you show me how to do that?" she said after he'd connected the first one.

Kyle was about to refuse her help, to say he could manage it alone, when he glimpsed the longing in her eyes. Again he wondered why a computer held such fascination for her.

"Please?" she asked.

"It's pretty easy. It's all color coded. Put the red plug in the red socket." He waited until she did that. "Now the green one to green. Now yellow."

With each step, Sara's smile widened. Kyle had never seen anyone find such pleasure in so simple a thing.

"There are no more colors," she told him. "Is it ready to go now?"

"No." He laughed at her frown. "That's only the first step. We still have to connect the speakers and then I have to program each computer."

"Oh." Disappointment dimmed her joy. "How many days will that take?"

"Days?" Kyle shook his head. "A few hours, maybe. Tell me what you know about computers, Sara."

"Nothing." She shrugged, looking embarrassed.

"I'll give you a crash course," Kyle said, suddenly feeling bad for her. "Computers are machines that have to be told what you want them to do. So I'm going to install programs that will do that. When I'm finished, they'll be ready to use."

"It sounds kind of complicated." Sara frowned.

"Well, I think making apple pies and soup and stew is complicated. Each of us has our own thing we're familiar with." Kyle continued explaining, but it wasn't long before he recognized Sara was totally lost.

He was feeling a little lost himself with that fresh lemon scent of her hair assailing his nostrils.

"Never mind. Once I get these running you'll understand better," he said, aware that Teddy sat silently listening across the room.

"I won't bother you. It's not fair for me to take up more of your time. Anyway, Rod has promised he will help me learn computers."

Kyle felt oddly disappointed but before he could puzzle out his feelings, Sara gasped.

"What's wrong?" Teddy asked, surging to his feet.

"The time," she said. "I must prepare lunch. You and Kyle will stay?"

Kyle opened his mouth to refuse but Teddy beat him to it.

"We'd love to stay for lunch." He grinned. "Kyle promised he'd feed me but he's not a very good cook. He says you are."

"That's nice of him." Sara's gaze met Kyle's then skittered away.

"Apple pie is my favorite," Teddy hinted.

"I'm afraid there isn't any left." Sara chuckled at Teddy's dejected expression. "But I'll think of something else for dessert today." She walked to the door, her steps quick and light. "We'll eat when Laurel returns. Let me know if you need anything."

"Thank you." Kyle waited until her footsteps died away before he turned back to the computer he'd been working on.

"Nice lady," Teddy mused.

"Very nice." Kyle struggled to focus his brain on booting up the computer and off Sara.

"What girl her age doesn't know about computers?" Teddy asked.

"I don't know. Something to do with her being in foster care, I think." Kyle scratched his head, trying to sort through the bits and pieces he knew about Sara and drawing a blank. "She hasn't told me much and I don't like to ask. Whenever she mentions the past, she gets this sad look as if it's painful to talk about."

"You should ask her. If it's painful, maybe it would help her to talk about it," Teddy said.

"Yeah," Kyle agreed. But the thought of such a personal conversation put a lump in his throat. He had a hundred questions rolling around his brain. As if he needed to think some more about Sara Kane. What he needed was to get back to his own life, not get more involved in hers. "I'm expecting some calls this afternoon about listing the house, so I have to get this finished and get home. Okay?"

"Sure. As long as we get to eat Sara's lunch before

we leave." Teddy rose. "I'll go outside and load up some of that junk from the renovations. I can haul it away this afternoon."

Despite Kyle's best efforts to remain focused as he worked, every so often Sara's face pushed its way into his mind until he acknowledged that he needed to know more about her. But how?

Rod wanted to create a website for wounded warriors to meet and share experiences. Personally Kyle had no desire to rehash his hellish memories, but maybe if he helped the boy, he could figure out why Sara Kane was so different from any other woman he'd ever met.

And maybe then he'd be able to figure out why he found her so appealing.

"I have never tasted anything so delicious, Sara. Thank you." Teddy accepted a third helping of lasagna, giving Sara a rush of satisfaction.

"I'm glad you like it." Her gaze rested on Laurel. Her boss had thanked Kyle effusively for the computers and then fallen strangely silent for the rest of the meal, very unlike the usually garrulous Laurel. In fact, every time she looked at Teddy, her blue eyes shot daggers at him.

"It is very good lasagna," Kyle agreed quietly. "Especially with the spinach."

"My way of sneaking vegetables into the boys. Would you like some more?" It was obvious to Sara that Laurel and Teddy had some issues between them, but since she didn't know anything about relationships, she doubted she could help.

"I've eaten plenty, thanks." Kyle's gaze slid from Teddy, to Laurel, then to her. "You're still intending on coming to the greenhouse this afternoon?"

"As soon as I finish cleaning up from lunch. Rod said he'd join me there. He has last period of class free and we want to get started." Sara knew they were just making conversation to cover the silence between the others, but the greenhouse was a connection between her and Kyle, making them cohorts of a sort. She liked that. "It's warmer today. I think I'll plant some lettuce seeds."

"Fresh lettuce, huh? That will be nice." Laurel glared at Teddy. "Not having to buy lettuce should cut our expenses, improve our bottom line."

Teddy bristled. "Look, Laurel, I didn't mean—"

"Excuse me. That's my phone." Laurel cut off Teddy's explanation and bolted from the room.

Kyle glanced at Sara and raised his eyebrows. Sara nodded. Something was definitely wrong between these two.

"I got some help with the expenses from Lucy, too," Sara said brightly, trying to lift the dark mood of the room. "Not only did she scrounge up those bikes for us to use, but her friend donated some rhubarb. I made a crisp for dessert."

"It sounds wonderful, but I guess I'm not as hungry as I thought." Teddy pushed away his plate. "I'll take that with me and eat it for dinner tonight. I should get going now."

"Of course. I'll wrap it up." Sara glanced at Kyle.

"I'd love some rhubarb crisp," he said. "But since Teddy's eager to get going and I caught a ride with him, maybe I could take some with me, also."

"Certainly." Sara wrapped generous portions for each man then walked them out. "I can't thank you enough for the computers, Kyle. I know the boys will be thrilled. And thank you, Teddy, for all your help, too."

"Rod can show you how to get online tonight," Kyle told her as he shrugged into his jacket. "You'll be an expert in no time."

"I'm not sure about that," she said. "But I'll try." Both men waved, climbed in Teddy's truck and drove away.

Sara closed the door and went to clean the kitchen. She found Laurel sitting at the table, her head in her hands.

"What's the matter?" Sara asked. She sat down, waiting for her friend to explain.

"It's that man," Laurel burst out. She lifted her head. Her face was red, her mouth pinched together in a tight line.

"Teddy? I could tell that there was something wrong between you two. But he's been such a help. He cleaned up that pile of garbage outside," she began.

"I don't care that he cleaned it up," Laurel snapped.

Sara had never seen Laurel so flustered. "I'm sorry, but I don't understand."

"I'm not sure I understand myself," Laurel admitted. "Teddy and I got off on the wrong foot. He's one of those men who has to be right, the kind who thinks he knows everything." She shook her head. "Forget it. I'm acting like a kid."

Sara was totally confused about relationships in general but this one in particular. By the time she thought of something to say it was too late.

"I have paperwork to do before I pick up the boys. I should get going," Laurel said as she left.

"See you later, then." Sara, totally muddled by Laurel, dragged on the coat Kyle had lent her and climbed on one of the bikes, wishing she had a clue how to help her friend. "Lord, I'm going to need some help to figure out this relationship business," she prayed as she rode into town.

By the time she arrived at Kyle's she was breathless from pedaling so hard because she couldn't rid her brain of thoughts of polar bears pursuing her. But a rush of joy bubbled inside her when she saw Kyle sitting in the sunshine.

"I thought you'd be having a nap after all your work this morning." She climbed off the bike, propped it up and walked into his yard. To her surprise, Kyle followed her into the greenhouse.

"I got tired of sorting through Dad's stuff so I thought I'd give you a hand out here."

"That's very nice of you, Kyle, but I didn't expect you to work on this. Rod and I can do it."

"I know you can." His now-familiar grin flashed. "I just need something to do, something physical," he amended. "I'm used to being on the go."

"By all means then, clean to your heart's content." In the warmth of the greenhouse, Sara took off her jacket and got to work, trying to ignore the fact that less than six feet away Kyle scrubbed and polished. She wasn't sure if she should talk to him or leave him be, but after a while, curiosity got the better of her. "Is there a lot of stuff you have to go through?"

"The usual accumulation, I guess." He rubbed particularly hard on one spot where Sara could see no dirt.

"It must be wonderful to look at his things and enjoy memories of happy times," she said.

"Not really." Kyle's voice sounded hard. "I look at his snowshoes and remember that I can't do that with him anymore. I can't do it by myself, either."

"No, you can't do that again. Yet. But you're alive," she said as gently as she could. "You can build new memories."

"How?"

"I don't know," she admitted honestly. "You'll have to ask God."

"Not gonna happen." He set down his cloth. "God and I don't talk."

There was a finality there that Sara couldn't argue with.

"Here comes Rod," Kyle said. He opened the door and greeted the boy. "I'll leave the two of you to finish. I'm going to tinker on my old ATV and see if I can get it ready to be sold."

"Thanks for your help." A part of her heart pinched as she watched Kyle walk away, broad shoulders bowed. He wasn't even going to try to use the machine. He was just going to let it go, let the past die as if it had never been.

Sara whispered a prayer. "Please help him."

Then she lifted her head and smiled at Rod. "I'm glad you're here," she said. "There's a lot of dirt that's accumulated."

Rod seemed to know what to do and they worked together for some time. Sara had no idea how long they'd been at it when Kyle yelled. When she saw him lying on the ground, her heart flew up into her throat. She dropped everything and ran.

"What's wrong? Did you hurt yourself?" When he simply lay there without answering, she demanded, "Kyle, what are you doing?"

"Admiring the clouds." He frowned at her. "What do you think I'm doing? I'm trying to figure out if I've broken something." He grunted as he sat up. "I might have left some bones intact," he muttered as he stretched. Rod held out a hand and Kyle grabbed it, using the boy's strength to leverage himself upright. "Thanks," he said.

Rod simply nodded then walked back inside the greenhouse.

"This thing is a heap of junk." He kicked his foot against one tire and winced. "I need a cup of coffee."

"We should go." Sara turned but froze when Kyle grabbed her arm.

"What I meant was, would you like a cup of coffee, too?" His gaze met hers and held.

"I guess I could. If you're sure you want me to."

"I'm sure, Sara. I'd like it very much." The sincerity in his voice convinced her he wanted company.

She checked her watch. She had time before she needed to start on dinner. "It's a lovely day. We could have it outside."

"If you want." Kyle wore a strange look. "Would you mind making it? Some things never change and I'm still lousy with coffee."

"So that's why you invited me." She laughed at his guilty look. "Just for that I should refuse."

"Please don't." He stood there, waiting, then lifted his eyebrows. "Please? I'd owe you one really big favor."

Like teaching her about the computer?

"Okay." She glanced toward Rod, thinking to ask if he wanted something to drink, but his attention was totally on the system that ventilated the greenhouse. Men. With a huff, Sara went inside. A moment later she had to laugh. As if she knew anything about men or how they thought.

It did feel nice to be needed, especially by Kyle because he always seemed so determined to be independent. It wasn't that she felt sorry for him. Kyle wasn't the kind of man who generated sympathy. It was more that she wanted to hear him laugh again, see joy fill his face.

Sara gulped at the strange sensations filling her. They made her nervous so she concentrated on the process of making the coffee, but in doing so she found the kitchen terribly confining. How could Kyle even get around? Everything seemed to be in the wrong place, in the way. A peek out the window told her Kyle and Rod were engaged, so Sara made her decision.

While the aroma of coffee grounds filled the room, she pushed and shoved, using every mite of strength she could summon. Five minutes later, she stood back, pleased with her efforts.

"How's that coffee— Oh." Kyle stood stock-still, taking in her changes.

"You don't like it," she guessed, watching emotions flicker across his face. "I'm sorry. I'll put it back, I promise."

"Wait. I think I can actually get around now." Kyle walked to the fridge, opened the door and shut it. He reached up to a cupboard and then pulled open the bottom drawer. "It works like a real kitchen should. It's the way it was when my mom was alive."

Sara flinched. Why hadn't she left well enough alone?

"This room came alive with her personality. She baked for everyone, everything." Kyle half smiled at Sara, lost in his memories. "After she died, Dad and I used it more as an office. He brought that armoire down here so he could do books for the business, but it should go back upstairs. It's too big for here."

Loath to break into his reminiscences, Sara waited several moments. He finally looked at her as if suddenly remembering where he was.

"The sun's gone, so we'll come in for coffee. Can you fill two of those yellow mugs? There's soda in the fridge for Rod. I'll call him."

Sara set his filled mug and Rod's soda on the table. When Rod and Kyle were seated, Sara sat, too, so Kyle wouldn't guess her mug was filled with water. Though she loved the scent of it brewing and enjoyed making it for others, she just didn't enjoy the taste.

"This is great coffee." Kyle savored a mouthful as he glanced around the room. "You know, maybe I should hire you to help me smarten the rest of the house up. That might help it sell faster."

Sell?

The bottom dropped out of her world. Sara set down her yellow cup and leaned back.

"You're selling your home?" she asked, trying to hide her surprise and shock.

"Yes, of course. I can't live in Churchill anymore," Kyle said in a matter-of-fact tone. "I'll clean up the place and hope to get a good dollar. Then I'll move."

Sara stared at her hands, devastated. She'd begun to think of Kyle as a friend, a very good friend. She'd even let herself daydream that maybe, perhaps, one day he could become more than that. Of course that was only a dream; it would never happen. But she had thought that with time she could help him break free of his bitterness toward God. Now he was saying they wouldn't have that time together.

Sara didn't want to examine the reasons why she found that depressing. She only knew she had to try to stop Kyle from leaving, not for herself but because she cared about him, and running away from his home, where his memories were etched into the Canadian north like long-ago carvings in the rock, wouldn't heal his hurting heart. Kyle had lived, loved, laughed and done everything here and she wanted him to do it again.

She wanted the very best for him. That was more important than any silly romantic daydreams. How could leaving be the best for him? And how could she deal with the sense of loss that even now enveloped her?

As Sara studied the man she'd come to respect

and admire, her head and her heart swirled with questions about Kyle Loness. None of which she had answers to.

Chapter Six

Kyle hadn't expected the call for help to come so soon.

"Whatever Sara did, the computer is totally whacked." Rod's voice gave little away.

"What's on the screen?" Kyle asked hopefully.

"It's black. Don't tell her I said this," Rod mumbled, "but Sara is about as good with a computer as I am with pie dough. She was checking out a website, last thing I knew. A few minutes later she yelled. By the time I got there her computer was dead."

"You don't know what she was doing?" Kyle clung to a fragment of hope that he wouldn't have to go out again today. His leg was aching and he'd hoped to relax.

"I haven't got a clue. I can usually figure out computer stuff but this time I'm stuck. Whatever she did, it shut down the system." Rod didn't sound hopeful.

"Are you in the computer room now?"

"Yes." Rod's flat tone held no hope.

"Let's try something." Kyle led him through several steps. Nothing worked. Finally he agreed to go to Lives.

"Please don't tell Sara I called you," Rod urged. "She really wants to get on the internet. But I'm afraid she'll try again on another computer and maybe knock out the entire network if you don't help me figure out what's wrong."

"I'll see if Teddy can drive me over." Kyle was curious about what was behind Sara's need to understand computers and get online. "Do you know why she's so eager to use the internet?"

"She's trying to find out about her family." A pause, then, "She's coming. I have to go." Rod hung up before Kyle could say any more.

He called Teddy, who reluctantly agreed to a second visit to Lives. While he waited for his ride, Kyle mused on what he'd learned.

Sara was a foster child. Now she was trying to find her family. That made sense if she'd been removed from her home as a young child. It might also explain why she was so curious about his past. Kyle remembered her appreciation of his home. Was that why she'd looked so devastated when he'd told her he was selling this place?

Because she didn't have a home of her own?

He recalled another of his father's favorite quotations, this time from Robert Frost. "Home is the place where, when you have to go there, They have to take you in." Though he'd moved around as a kid, Kyle had always had a home.

Apparently Sara had not enjoyed the same security.

Hearing the low growl of Teddy's engine outside, Kyle tugged on his coat and walked out of the house. Sometime yesterday, Hector had managed to build a ramp, making it much easier to leave the house. Kyle made a mental note to buy the man dinner as thanks as he climbed inside the truck.

"What's the emergency?" Teddy demanded.

"Sara killed one of the computers."

"Already?" Teddy's eyes widened.

"Yes, but you can't say anything," Kyle insisted. "I'm going to pretend we stopped by to make sure everything's okay with them. You good with that?"

Teddy shrugged.

"Apparently Sara is upset. She blames herself for the crash."

"Is Laurel going to be there?" Teddy asked in a low tone.

"I imagine so." Kyle studied his friend. "Is that a problem?"

"Not as long as I don't run into her." Teddy grimaced. "I know what you're going to say."

Kyle inclined his head to one side, curious to see if Teddy knew him as well as he thought.

"You'll say let it go. I'm trying." Teddy tossed him a sideways glance. "May I suggest you do the same?"

"I don't know what you're talking about." Kyle stared out the window. "I'm not the one who's feuding with the woman who runs Lives."

"To clarify, I'm not exactly feuding with Laurel Quinn, but that isn't what I meant." Teddy was silent until they turned into the driveway of Lives. "I meant that chip on your shoulder."

"You're seeing chips where there aren't any." Kyle grasped the door handle but Teddy's grip made him pause.

"You're going to tell me you're not mad at God or at that woman who dumped you?" Teddy nodded when Kyle didn't respond. "That's what I'm talking about. You have to let it go."

"You expect me to accept that God chose to kill my father two weeks before I was to come home?" Kyle barked a harsh laugh. "I should pretend that's okay with me?"

"You're making it sound like God reached out and struck him dead," Teddy argued. "Your dad had a heart attack, Kyle."

"Which God could have prevented. At least until I got home. But He didn't." Kyle exhaled.

"It was hard for me to accept your father's death, too," Teddy said. "But ultimately I am not in charge of the world. God is. As His child, I accept that He knows what He's doing."

"That's a cop-out." Kyle shoved the door open and awkwardly climbed out.

"Is it?" Teddy walked with him to the door. "I don't understand astrophysics or space sciences. Does that mean it's a cop-out if I accept it when they tell me there is no life on the moon?"

"It's not the same."

"Sure it is." Teddy's lips lifted. "I'm telling you, buddy, if you don't knock that chip off your shoulder, you'll miss what's right in front of you."

"Which is?" Kyle asked, though he wasn't sure he wanted to know.

"Sara." Teddy's smirk said it all.

The door opened before Kyle could respond.

"Hi, Laurel," he said.

"Wow!" Laurel grinned at him. "Your sense of smell must be incredible." She shot a glare at Teddy but stood back to allow them both to enter.

"My sense of smell?" As soon as he said it, Kyle knew what she was talking about. The aroma of freshly made popcorn filled the room, combined with—caramel?

"Sara's just made some special popcorn for our movie night. You're welcome to join us. I'm sure the movie will be to your taste—action adventure with lots of car chases. The guys chose it."

"Sounds great." Kyle walked to the door of the family room and smiled at the group of boys. Then he turned back to Laurel. "Actually we just came to check if the computers are working properly. Sometimes there are hiccups with new systems."

"That's very kind of you. Boys, this is the man who kindly donated those new computers for you to use." She waited until the yells of "thanks, man" ended. "Do we have an issue with the computers?" she asked, glancing around the room.

Kyle waited but no one said anything, including Rod, who seemed intent on staring at the floor. A moment later, Sara stepped forward, wearing a red-checked apron and holding a wooden spoon in one hand.

"I broke one," she admitted with a red face.

"Good thing we stopped by, then," Kyle said with a warning glance at Teddy. "I'll go check it out."

"Need any help?" Laurel asked.

"Uh—" He struggled with an appropriate way to refuse Laurel's offer.

"I wasn't talking about me." She laughed self-deprecatingly. "I thought maybe Rod could help you. He seems to be the most computer literate among us."

Rod didn't say anything. But he rose to lead the way toward the computer room. Laurel, after a sideways glance at Teddy, flopped down in a chair in the family room.

"I'll stay here. I'm partial to Sara's special popcorn." Teddy flopped down in the chair Rod had just vacated. "Actually I'm partial to anything Sara makes."

The boys hooted with laughter as Sara's cheeks pinked even more.

"Save me some," Kyle said before he left.

Rod was waiting for him in the computer room. "It's this one," he said, taking the chair in the next station.

Kyle tested the connection, the switch and several other possibilities before typing in commands. Nothing happened. "Huh. That's weird."

"It's ruined, isn't it?" Sara stood behind them, her hands twisting together.

"No, Sara, I'm sure it's not." Kyle was touched by the concern in her eyes.

"Then what's wrong with it?" She didn't wait for an answer. "I knew I shouldn't have used it. Rod thought I'd be fine, but I have no idea what I'm doing. I've ruined your lovely gift and now the boys will suffer." Tears glittered in her lashes.

"Sara." Kyle waited until she looked directly at him. "It's not broken. Computers get glitches. Sometimes they refuse to do something. Stop worrying. We'll figure it out."

"Okay." A flicker of relief lightened her gray eyes.

"Now, can you tell me what you were doing?" he asked. "Do you remember?"

"I was looking at—do you call it a page?" She waited for his nod. "Rod said if something was underlined it meant there was more information. So I clicked on a word. A bunch of things started flashing on the screen. I couldn't stop them no matter how often I clicked on the back arrow." She turned to Rod. "I remembered you told me that's how I should get back to where I was. It didn't work. I touched a key and everything went black."

Rod nodded. His gaze met Kyle's.

"You thinking what I'm thinking?" Kyle asked.

"A virus. But how did it get around the protection?" Rod frowned.

"What's a virus?" Sara asked.

Rod explained while Kyle worked. But no matter what he tried the computer did not respond.

"Maybe this machine's a dud," Rod mused.

"Let's open it up." With Rod's help, Kyle removed the back. He was too conscious of Sara watching every move, her soft lemon scent filling his nostrils. Maybe that was why he missed the most obvious solution.

"Look." Rod pointed to the loose cord connection.

"I don't understand how that happened. Or why it suddenly became an issue." Kyle reset the component and pressed the power button. The computer immediately hummed to life. Once the normal screen was visible, Kyle ran a diagnostics test. Everything seemed to be fine. "Now you try using the internet," he said to Sara. He rose from his seat.

Sara backed away. "I'll ruin it," she said.

"It wasn't anything you did. It was a loose connection. That's fixed now." He smiled at her. "Go ahead and try it."

"Do you mind if I leave?" Rod asked. "I want to see the movie."

"Yes, go, Rod. Please. You've spent enough time on me." Sara grimaced.

"Go, Rod. I'll teach her." Kyle knew he was doing what he'd told himself not to do. He was getting involved. But Rod said Sara wanted to find her family. He couldn't walk away from that. "Okay. Tell me what you want to know."

"It's silly." She avoided his gaze.

"Nothing's silly. The internet is loaded with information. Let's find what you need."

"I want to find my family," she said after studying him for a minute.

"Okay, then." Kyle pulled up a chair beside her, trying to ignore the soft feelings her look of gratitude caused. He couldn't ignore her beauty so easily and got caught up in the stare from her lovely silver-gray eyes.

Time lapsed until Kyle realized his thoughts had strayed to her full pink lips, imagining what kissing them would be like. He coughed, straightened and forced himself to focus. "Let's start with a search on last names. Go ahead."

Each time she tried to give up, he refused to let her. Gently, tenderly he repeated the steps that would lead her to find what she wanted. He returned her grin when at last her search returned results. "See? You can do it."

"With your help. Thank you for being so patient." Her smile blazed away his shadows.

Kyle basked in that smile for a few minutes before he got his senses under control by reminding himself of his intent. He was leaving Churchill. He was going to find a place where he could do something he loved. The fact that he had no idea exactly what that something might be nagged at him. But Kyle ignored it, just as he ignored the flutter of awareness that rushed through him when Sara hit the wrong keys and, to redirect her, he covered her hand with his without thinking about what he was doing.

"There's not much here," she said, obviously disappointed.

"Now we have to go a step deeper," he told her, hating that sad tone in her usually musical voice. "Can you add anything to the information you've already given?"

"My mother's name is Sophia," she said, apparently unaware of the effect she had on him.

The lemon scent of her hair, the softness of her skin when her hand brushed his, the little gasps she made when something new filled the screen all contributed to breaking his concentration.

"Should I type in her whole name?"

"Can't hurt to try." He waited while she did. "That's what searching the web is about, Sara. Keep putting in information, asking questions. Eventually you'll find something that will lead you to the next step."

"Yes, I see." She gazed at him. "Thank you, Kyle."

That sweet smile, those incredible eyes—Kyle suddenly knew that it wasn't going to be easy to remain uninvolved.

Sara Kane was a very lovable woman.

But he'd met lovable before and it had let him down. He'd learned that lesson and faced the shame of it. No way was he going to repeat the experience.

Don't get involved, he told himself.

You already are, his brain mocked.

He ignored that little voice and concentrated on showing Sara everything she needed to know.

"I did it, Laurel." Sara felt like crowing with triumph. She slid the last pan of apple strudel in the oven.

"Hmm? Did what?" Laurel blinked at her as if she hadn't heard a word.

"You're tired. You should have slept in," Sara told her. "Teddy said that's what Saturdays are for."

"Maybe Teddy can afford to sleep in. He doesn't have this place to run. Not that he wouldn't like to," she added in a cranky voice. "He's always trying to boss me around." Laurel's forehead creased in a frown.

"Really?" Sara frowned. "I didn't notice that.

Well, he's being helpful. What's wrong between you two, anyway?"

"He tried to stop Lives," Laurel said, her face tightening. "He talked to town council about it without consulting me first." She shook her head. "Whenever I look at him I remember that and the gossip his interference caused. It makes me furious."

"Well, I think he's over that. He's a nice man and he's trying to help us. So is Kyle." Sara blushed at Laurel's searching glance. "Last night he helped me search for my mother online. I even learned how to send an email," she said, proud of her accomplishments.

"Good for you. You got a response to that letter you sent about your mom. Wasn't that helpful?"

"Not really. They said the records are sealed unless I get her permission. But how can I get her permission if I can't find her?" Sara shook her head. "It's very frustrating."

"I'm sure it is. But don't give up. Maybe with Kyle's help, you'll find her or your father." Laurel yawned again. "I'm going to work outside today. Teddy told me all that scrap metal someone left behind can be sold. We could use the money."

"I've been thinking." Sara paused, unsure about offering her opinion.

"About what?" Laurel said. "You're a part of Lives, Sara. I appreciate your input."

"Well, I was wondering if we should have an open house. To show people in Churchill what we're about." She hesitated then explained. "When I was coming back from the greenhouse the other day, I heard some women talking. They think the kids are dangerous. Maybe if they saw what Lives looks like, they'd feel more at ease, even offer to help us occasionally."

"If people think that, it's Teddy Stonechild's fault." Laurel's tone was blistering. "He fostered so many rumors about this place, I had to keep reassuring them to get them to even consider allowing me to open. I suppose he's complaining about my management again."

"I doubt that, but it doesn't matter, Laurel. What matters is how we get the town's support." Sara thought for a moment. "We could do it next Saturday, offer coffee and stuff that I'd bake. Nobody could take offense if they're sitting around chatting."

Laurel was silent.

"It was just an idea. You probably have something else in mind." Sara shrugged.

"It's brilliant. You are a genius." Laurel hugged her so tightly she squeezed out Sara's breath. "Can you make enough pies?"

"Why pies?" Sara asked.

"Because the men will come for sure if there are pies." She chuckled then sobered. "But will this interfere in your work in the greenhouse? I know that's important to you."

"Rod and I have planted a few seeds," Sara explained. "But we're waiting until it warms up a bit. Kyle's mom wrote the best planting time is the first week of June."

Laurel gave her a speculative look. "You're fond of Kyle, aren't you?"

"I like him. Is that what you mean?" At Laurel's silence, Sara looked up from her work.

"Actually I was wondering if you and he were romantically attracted to each other."

Sara stared at her. Then she began to laugh.

"What's so funny?" Laurel demanded. "Women are attracted to men, you know."

"It's funny because no one would be attracted to me." Sara rolled her eyes. "I don't know anything about men, but I would think they'd be attracted to girls who know things, who understand and enjoy the same things they do."

"Sweetie, you are beautiful and smart. And you know plenty of things, which is why you run this place as well as you do."

"That's nice of you to say." Sara tucked away the compliment.

"I'm not being nice," Laurel said firmly. "I'm being

truthful. In my experience, men like women who enjoy life. That's you, Sara. You enjoy everything."

"Cooking for those you love—what's not to like?" Sara asked in all seriousness, surprised when Laurel exploded with laughter. "Anyway, you're wrong about Kyle. He isn't attracted to me. He's not even going to stay in Churchill. He's going to sell his home."

"Really?" Laurel asked.

"Yes." Sadness filled Sara. "He doesn't think he can stay here and still have a full life. I wish he'd see all the things he can do instead of all the things he can't."

"Maybe you can show him."

"I'd like to," Sara said, studying her friend. "But how?"

"I don't know. Maybe if you got him to try some of the things he used to love."

"That's too big a step right now," Sara said, certain that Kyle wouldn't even consider it. "But maybe if I could get him talking—" She fell into thought.

"You're planning something, aren't you?" Laurel smiled. "I know that look."

"I'm planning to have guests tomorrow. A Sunday lunch after church, like roast beef and mashed potatoes. And pie," she added with a twinkle. "Perhaps lemon?"

Laurel smiled. "And who are we inviting to this meal? Lucy and Hector?"

"Of course." Sara smiled. "After all their help, that would be natural. And Teddy, of course."

"Oh, why him?" Laurel's face lost its mirth.

"You can hardly deny he's been a great help to us," Sara reasoned. "Just removing that pile of junk makes Lives look so much better. You said it yourself—we'll take all the help we can get."

"But that's not the reason, is it?"

"Of course not." Sara spared a moment to imagine her friend with someone special in her life.

"You're not—" Laurel hesitated. "You're not trying to matchmake, are you? Because I am in no way interested in Teddy Stonechild."

"I wouldn't dream of playing matchmaker." Sara covered her burning cheeks with her hands. "I don't know anything about that," she admitted.

"Then…" Laurel raised one eyebrow.

"My thought is that if we could all get together over a meal, perhaps the boys would ask some questions of Kyle and he would tell us what it was like to be raised here."

"Sounds reasonable," Laurel agreed. "But what's the point?"

"If Kyle could speak about the past, share his best memories of living here," Sara said, "maybe it would spark some desire to stay here."

"Why does it matter to you so much, sweetie?" Laurel's lips curved in a smile.

"Because he doesn't have anywhere to go," Sara burst out. "Kyle's running away from here and from his anger at God over his father's death. But he doesn't know where to go and he doesn't realize that life won't be any easier for him away from Churchill. When he sells his house he'll have nothing left of his past or his family. I don't want him to give that up without counting the cost."

Laurel whistled.

"What?" Sara asked.

"I'm amazed by your ability to see the hurt in people's hearts." Laurel hugged her close. "I've known psychiatrists who couldn't have diagnosed Kyle's hurt as well as you."

"I just don't want Kyle to keep blaming God," Sara said, embarrassed by the praise.

"As I said, a very clever woman." Laurel let her go. "Sunday lunch is what we'll have. And next Saturday is going to be the grand opening at Lives Under Construction. Tomorrow we'll ask our friends to help us put on a day like Churchill hasn't seen for a long time. We'll invite anyone who wants to come."

"Do you think Kyle will come?" Sara asked anxiously.

"I think you'll probably have to persuade him," Laurel answered honestly.

"Then that's what I'll do. But I'll pray for help." Sara couldn't keep the smile she felt inside from showing.

Feeling positive about her plans, Sara decided to try her hand at another internet search. She logged in as Kyle had shown her then typed in her mother's name and a bunch of—what did he call them?—hits, a bunch of hits appeared.

"Please help me find her," she prayed. But an hour later, she was no further ahead. She clicked off the screen. Maybe tomorrow she'd ask Kyle if there was a way to narrow the search even more.

It occurred to Sara then that she was running to Kyle with a lot of her problems. But that was only temporary. She'd soon learn how to search on her own.

In the meantime, she was going to use every interaction with him that she could to try to get him to rethink his anger at God and his future. After all, she was concerned about him and his insistence on self-reliance. She felt he used it to isolate himself. He needed her help.

Really?

Or was it that she needed to help him to satisfy the longing in her heart to see him whole, healed and fully engaged in life.

And then he'll leave, her head reminded her. A pang of loss shot through her but Sara focused on something else, something that chewed at her.

Why did helping Kyle matter so much?

In the silence of the kitchen Sara searched her heart. She couldn't help but acknowledge that helping Kyle eased that longing in her heart to be special to someone.

It wasn't only friendship she felt for Kyle. But what exactly was it?

Chapter Seven

"So that's what we're planning." Sara cupped her mug of hot chocolate, head tilted to one side as she waited for his response.

"A grand opening, huh?" Kyle finished filling the little peat pots lined up on the greenhouse shelf. Then he picked up his own mug. Sara followed him outside to the two chairs he'd placed in a patch of sun beside the house. The warmth told him summer was definitely on the way.

"Well?" she prodded.

"A grand opening is a good idea," he admitted. Funny how he'd learned to discern the nuances in Sara's voice; she sounded nervous.

"God is blessing us at Lives. We want the community to share that. So would you like to take part in our opening?" Sara asked.

Blessing? God was blessing Lives? Given that Kyle had witnessed a major plumbing issue while he was enjoying Sunday lunch today, he was of the opinion that God had messed up in the blessings department. But he wasn't about to argue with Sara. He was weary of hearing her harp on the subject of God's goodness.

"Why me? I don't have anything to do with Lives."

"You've had a great deal to do with it, and you're welcome to have more." Her smile teased him. "As much as you want."

"Sara, I'm happy for you to use the greenhouse and I'm glad if the computers are of some help and I was happy to talk about my experiences living here with the kids the other day at lunch. I hope it helped them."

"I think it did," she said, eyes shining. "The way you talk about tracking animals, going on expeditions, even watching the polar bears and their cubs, that was amazing. I think we all felt like we were right there with you."

"That's nice," he said, feeling trapped. "Thank you for saying that. But I've got to get ready to move." She was getting too close. That intense silver-gray scrutiny of hers saw too much and that made Kyle antsy. "I have a lot to sort through."

"I can help you," she offered.

A heartfelt no almost spilled from Kyle's lips, but he didn't say it. It would seem as though he was throwing her generosity back in her face, and he couldn't bring himself to do that. Yet he desperately wanted Sara to understand he could manage alone.

"Where would you start?"

"I don't know." Kyle weighed the negatives of letting her help. She'd be in his space again. And she'd leave her mark there. Even out here, in the fresh air, he was still inundated with that lemon scent of her hair.

He ignored the voice in his head telling him to reject her offer.

"In the living room?" he suggested.

"Okay." She drained her mug then jumped up, obviously excited. "I've got two hours before I have to get back. We can get a lot accomplished in that time."

"Sure." Kyle led the way inside, certain he'd lost his mind in agreeing to let her help. "Where would you like to start?" Sara asked, her lips tipped up in an eager smile.

Kyle glanced around the room, which bulged with the paraphernalia of his father's life, and again felt grief's familiar weight.

"Let's start with the magazines," Sara suggested.

He checked to see if she sensed he was about to recant. But as usual, Sara was focused on the job to be done. Again his curiosity about her past bubbled up. What made her so driven? He was going to ask but Sara was all business.

"The hospital would love these magazines for their waiting room. We'll throw out the oldest ones."

"I'll do that." Kyle could deal with magazines and newspapers, even if they were of the hunting and fishing variety, which his father had loved.

"Okay. I'll collect all the knickknacks so you can decide which to keep." Sara placed the objects on the square glass coffee table where Kyle had colored as a child, humming as she worked.

Kyle knew the song. *This is the day that the Lord hath made.* It was from Psalms.

"Your father must have loved animals." She held up the intricate carving of a walrus in her palm. "This is exquisite."

"When I was a kid, a chief of a Native tribe gave it as a gift after Dad rescued his daughter."

Kyle was surprised when she recognized the artist.

"I saw his work in a Vancouver gallery," Sara explained. She gazed at him in that starry-eyed fashion of hers. "He's one of Canada's foremost sculptors. You were so blessed to live here, Kyle."

Blessed? As a kid, maybe. Not so much now, he thought.

"I think God puts us where we can learn so that when we are in hard places, we have something to fall back on. Don't you?"

Kyle pinched his lips together as he loaded the last of the magazines into a box.

"I love to hear Lucy's missionary stories." Sara dusted each item and the crevice where it had lived. "Her stories remind me over and over that God is always with us."

Kyle couldn't stop the rush of words that tumbled out. "I don't believe that."

"I guess it's hard to believe when things seem really bad." The cloud in her eyes dimmed Sara's joy, but just for a moment. The shadows disappeared as quickly as they'd come. "But it's true. The Bible tells us that."

"And you believe everything the Bible says?" he demanded.

"Don't you?" a wide-eyed Sara asked.

"Not anymore." Kyle grunted when his shin bumped into one of the three recliners in the room. "This should have been trashed long ago."

"I guess your dad loved it." Sara hummed "Heavenly Sunshine" now.

"My mom used to sit in this old chair," he mused to himself. "She loved to knit here, in front of the window."

"Then there's your answer," Sara said. "The chair probably helped your dad remember the good times with her. Sometimes God uses memories to comfort us."

"Sara, stop!" Kyle yelled. Her response infuriated him. "Stop telling me how good God is, how wonderful God is, how much He cares for us. I don't want to hear it."

She looked as if he'd slapped her. Tears welled in her amazing eyes. She made no attempt to rub them away. "I'm s-sorry, Kyle," she stammered.

"So am I. But I can't take it anymore." He moderated his voice but wouldn't back down. "I can't hear about God's goodness while I'm emptying out this house my father loved."

"Kyle—" She reached out a hand.

"No." He jerked away from her and almost lost his balance, which made him even angrier. "You believe anything you want, but you can't convince me that God did the right thing by letting my dad die. Don't even try."

Sara turned away and pretended to clean another shelf, but he knew by her sniffing that she was weeping.

The next few minutes seemed like hours. Sara worked but not with the joy she'd shown before. Before she'd seemed tough, resilient and strong enough to weather anything, but she didn't look strong now. She looked beaten.

He'd done that to her.

That was when it dawned on Kyle that Sara's gutsy exterior hid a deep vulnerability. Why was that? What in the past had hurt her?

He had a hunch it had to do with her foster-care

years and made a vow to find out, but not now. He'd hurt her now.

If you hurt someone, Kyle, you have to make it right. His father's voice shamed him.

"Sara, I'm sorry," he said, trying to coax her to face him. "I wasn't trying to hurt you or demean your faith." He swallowed the lump in his throat. "It's just—I'm not where you are right now. I don't know if I ever will be again. I feel betrayed."

"God doesn't betray us, Kyle. Not ever." She moved to the side table where his father's Bible lay open. She fingered the pages for a few moments. When she finally spoke she said, "God is good. He cannot be otherwise. From what I've heard of your father, I believe he knew that. I also believe he is at peace with God. All his questions have been answered."

"Well, mine haven't," Kyle snapped back.

"God is ready and willing to listen to your questions, Kyle." She lifted her head to study him. "All you have to do is ask them." She touched his arm with the very tips of her fingers and then got back to work.

As Kyle watched her, a new thought crept into his brain. What would it be like to have Sara nearby to confide in? How would it feel to know she was there for him all the time?

Kyle immediately rejected that. He'd resolved not

to allow any involvement in his life. He wasn't going to be staying in Churchill, anyway.

But even if he did, what would Sara get out of a relationship with him?

The answer hit hard—a life with a cripple.

Kyle was older than Sara, but it was the kind of age that came from much more than just years. Besides, he had a hunch she was running from something herself.

In that moment Kyle realized that maybe *he* could help *her*. He'd been selfish, self-involved and thinking only of himself. He'd willingly accepted every time she offered help, but what had he given back to her?

"I have to go now, Kyle. But I was wondering…" Sara bit her bottom lip in hesitation. Then, before his eyes, her resolve moved in. "Will you take part in our grand opening ceremonies?"

"Just a small part," he finally agreed. He owed her that at least, for making her weep.

"Great!" She threw her arms around him and hugged him, then quickly pulled away, almost costing him his balance. Her sunny smile sent a shaft of warmth straight to his heart. "See you tomorrow."

Kyle said goodbye to her, but it was long after Sara Kane had left his house. Half-bemused by the rush of yearning she'd left behind, he slowly boxed up the trinkets she'd laid across the table, keeping only three that were precious to him. He hauled the magazines to the trash and put the newer ones on the back step. He'd ask Teddy to take those to the hospital, as Sara had suggested.

But even an hour later, the question foremost on Kyle's mind just wouldn't go away.

Who is Sara Kane?

He could have found a way to ask her, but it seemed intrusive. Besides, he didn't want to know more about this disturbing woman. She was in his thoughts enough without adding to it. Besides, what if it included a man who'd hurt her? How could he respond to that? Or what if he did ask her and she mistook his question? What if she thought—well, the wrong thing. Like he was interested in her or something.

Aren't you?

Kyle's brain swirled with a thousand reasons why it would be a bad idea to ask Sara about her past. And for every reason the question hung in his brain, his need to know grew.

Who was Sara Kane?

Ignoring the work he'd hoped to do before the real-estate agent's visit on Tuesday, Kyle finally sat down at his dad's desk and booted up his laptop. The cursor blinked at him, waiting. His little finger hovered over the enter key. One click, that was all it would take to find out more about her. One click.

Sara's expressions—happy, sad, excited, worried, troubled—all of them passed through Kyle's mind.

Sara, who worked so hard to make others happy. Sara, who always tiptoed lightly around others' feelings. How had she become that way?

Kyle wasn't aware of the passage of time until suddenly, as the moody shadows of the evening filled the room, he knew he couldn't do it. He couldn't pry into her past. Not yet.

He'd win her trust and learn her story the old-fashioned way: by talking to her himself. Lives' grand opening offered the perfect opportunity.

"I can't believe I agreed to cut the ribbon."

Kyle studied the throngs of people who'd shown up for the grand opening of Lives Under Construction.

"The persuasion of a woman is a powerful thing," Teddy agreed. "Especially if that woman has an innocent, vulnerable look like our Sara."

"Our Sara?" Kyle frowned.

"Haven't you noticed?" Teddy asked. "The whole town's adopted her. You're not the only one who cares about her."

Kyle took a second look at his friend's face. Something unspoken lingered under those words, some hint that suggested there was more to his appearance here today than a simple favor.

"I do care about her—as her friend."

"Did I say differently?" Teddy smiled the smug grin Kyle hated.

"No. You implied it." He glared at the big man. "You think I'm doing this because I've got some kind of a crush on Sara Kane?"

"There's that chip on your shoulder again." With a look that said he'd been maligned, Teddy moved to greet one of the town's council members.

Kyle knew Teddy was hinting that he was getting involved.

"You look good," Sara said as her eyes scanned him, taking in every detail. "I'm sure you look amazing in your uniform, too." Surely she hadn't overheard his conversation with Teddy.

"It's—uh, at the cleaners." *Stupid.* There was no dry cleaner's in Churchill. He licked his lips and swallowed nervously.

"Do all these people bother you?" She patted his arm, her sunny smile warming him. "Don't worry. Once we get started it won't take a minute for the mayor to declare Lives is officially open. Then you can disappear if you want."

"Sure." Kyle didn't explain his worry that the mayor would make some reference to him being a veteran and draw attention to his damaged leg. "It's a pretty good turnout."

"Curiosity is a powerful motivator," she murmured, again revealing her insightful nature. "I only hope I have enough food."

"Are you kidding?" Kyle had seen the long tables

with their pristine white cloths and the trays of edibles. "You've got enough to feed an army."

"Thank you, Kyle." Her smile flashed as she touched his arm again. "You always know how to cheer me up."

"Any news about your mom?" He asked mostly to get his focus off the tingle of her touch. When the joy leeched from her face, he wished he'd kept his mouth shut.

"No. I haven't been able to find anything." The glow in her silver-gray eyes dimmed. "I don't know what else to try."

"Maybe when this is over, we could take another stab at it," he offered. Then he wondered why he'd made the gesture. He didn't want to get more involved in Sara's life. He'd deliberately stayed away from Lives this past week as much as possible for just that reason.

But the sadness on her face made him want to help.

"Are you sure you wouldn't mind, Kyle?" The sparkle returned to her eyes, picking up the glints of silver in the scarf she wore knotted at her neck. Her voice was full of hope. "Really?"

"I wouldn't mind," he told her, mesmerized by her gorgeous smile.

"Thank you."

"Sara, I have to ask. What happens if you can't find your mother?"

"Then I look for my father." She fixed him with her gaze. "I have to find my family, Kyle. It doesn't matter where they are or what happened to them, or why they left me. I have to find them."

"Good for you." He saw Laurel marshaling the various dignitaries to get them on the little platform. Kyle had to get up there before things started. He wasn't about to let the entire town see the gimp stumble, or even worse, trip. "I'll talk to you later," he said.

"You will." Sara's eyes held his for a moment before he drew away.

Because she was watching, Kyle forced himself to walk without the limp that usually accompanied his steps. He made it to the platform and negotiated his way onto it without mishap. Jubilant, he stood exactly where Laurel told him to and faced the crowd. Thankfully her speech was short.

"I'm delighted to welcome you here today. Our children are our future. But how can they build that future unless they learn to reject the violence that is so pervasive in our world? Our goal at Lives Under Construction is to show those who come here that there is a better way, a way that they will find if we stand beside them, guiding them, showing them love for themselves and for others. Thank you."

The mayor then stepped forward and gave his short speech with no mention of Kyle, to his relief. Then the president of the chamber of commerce announced, "I hereby declare that Lives Under Construction is officially open."

On cue, Kyle stepped forward and snipped the ribbon held by the dignitaries. A burst of clapping ensued.

"Please join us in celebrating our grand opening," Laurel said, indicating the tables of tea, coffee and punch, which the boys manned.

People began chatting with their neighbors. Laurel thanked Kyle for his help then hurried away to make sure her students were doing their jobs properly.

"Good work, Kyle," Sara said, grinning. "You could be a professional ribbon cutter."

"Yeah," he said, wondering if that was all he was good for now. Caught in his thoughts, he stepped off the platform onto a bit of spongy rock moss he'd specifically avoided earlier. His knee buckled and in a flash, Kyle was flat on his backside with the whole world watching.

Furious with himself, he struggled to rise but his prosthesis inhibited his movements.

Without a word, Sara slid her arm under his shoulder and around his back. "Lean on me, Kyle," she murmured.

Pain radiated through his hip and down to his stump. He could hardly breathe for the agonizing spears that shot through his body. Somehow Sara managed to get him upright. He felt rather than saw her motion with her hand. A moment later three of the boys clustered around him, shielding him from the onlookers.

Then Kyle heard shy, quiet Rod say in a loud voice meant to carry, "There's pie, lots of it. Lemon and apple and chocolate."

The crowd shifted like a school of fish, their interest in Kyle forgotten.

"Inside," Sara said to the boys. "Let's use the side entrance. It's closer and we don't have to go through the crowd."

"I'm going home," Kyle argued, furious at his weakness. "Get Teddy."

"Teddy's holding court, creating a diversion. Use it," Sara ordered. Her implacable expression brooked no discussion. "Use us to walk, Kyle."

"Wonderful idea," he puffed, trying to spare her his weight and unable to do even that. "Wish I could do it. But thanks to God, I can't even walk anymore."

Sara glanced at him but said nothing more until he was inside and seated on a chair in the computer room. She got his leg straightened and resting on a stool, then sent the boys back outside, except for Tony, their newest arrival, who'd flown in just yesterday. She ordered him to bring ice and a towel. When he'd left and the two of them were alone, Sara clamped her hands on her hips and glared at him.

"You blame everything on God, don't you, Kyle?" He'd never heard her voice so harsh.

"He could have—"

She didn't let him finish.

"Yes, yes. God could have kept your father alive, He could have saved you from losing your leg and He could have kept my family together." Sara bent, placed her hands on the arms of the chair Kyle was sitting in and leaned forward until her face was within inches of his. "But He didn't."

"Exactly." He leaned back, thinking he'd proven his point.

But Sara was just getting started.

"So what are you going to do now?" she demanded. "Spend the rest of your life blaming Him?"

"I don't have any rest of my life," Kyle snarled. "My life is over."

"Really?" Her fingers slid around his wrist. "There's still a pulse."

"My life is over, Sara," he repeated. "Why can't you accept that?"

"Because it isn't true." She drew another chair forward and sat in it, facing him but farther away, for which Kyle was thankful. Her nearness, as usual, did odd things to his heartbeat. "I'll accept that your life *as you knew it* is over. Now it's time to reinvent yourself."

"As what? A cripple who can't even stand up in public? As the guy everyone feels sorry for? Embarrass myself like that again?" He clenched his jaw and shook his head. "Sorry, can't do that. Won't do that."

"That isn't what I meant and you know it. But a little embarrassment isn't the worst thing that could happen to you." She took the ice and towel Tony brought, made a pack and placed it on the exact spot where the pain was the greatest.

As the chill penetrated the pain, Kyle wondered how she knew exactly where to put the ice pack.

"I've got to get back out there," she said. "Laurel is counting on me to keep the food coming. Can we talk about this later?"

"I doubt it." He tried not to show how much pain he was in. "If I ever imagined, even for a minute, that I could be a contributor to this community, that dream was smashed out there. I can't even stand up."

"We all trip at some time in our lives. Maybe you should let yourself lean on us while you try harder." Sara's amazing eyes held him in their grip for several moments. Then she rose, smoothed her plain black skirt and straightened her shoulders. "Stay here. Tony will get you whatever you need. I'll see you later."

Furious at her intimation that he'd given up too easily, Kyle waited until she was almost out the door before he spoke again.

"You want me to start over, Sara? Well, I'm going to do exactly that. Just as soon as I sell the house."

Sara paused for one infinitesimal moment then kept walking.

Anger seared through him. Why couldn't she understand? Why couldn't anyone understand what he'd lost?

"Help me get out of here," he said to Tony, but the boy shook his head.

"I haven't been here long but I know one thing. Sara says you stay then you stay," he said. "Want to play checkers?"

Kyle wanted to explode at him. But what good would that do? He shook his head.

Tony watched him for a moment then sat across from him. "Can I ask you something?"

"I suppose." Why had he ever agreed to come here today?

"At school they told us there are polar bears around here." Tony studied him. "Did you ever see one?"

"Sure." Kyle shrugged. "My dad and I used to take tourists to see them. The ice is pretty much gone from the bay now, so most of the bears are gone, too. I don't think you have to worry about running into one."

"I'm not worried. I'd like to run into one. I want to know what they're like."

Kyle frowned. "Why?" he demanded.

"My grandmother was Inuit. She's gone now, but she used to tell us stories about Mother Bear. I wish I'd listened better." Tony's expression was filled with sorrow. "I thought I hated being part Inuit but it's like hating a part of myself. You know?"

"Yeah, I know." He adjusted his ice pack. "My dad knew a lot of the old stories."

"Can you tell me some of them?" Tony begged.

Seeing the keen interest on the boy's face, Kyle launched into the first story that came to mind. As he began, he was besieged by memories of the intonation of his father's voice. But then the power his father had infused into the story took over and he strove to do justice to the moral of the tale.

For the first time in months, some of the joy Kyle had felt before he'd left home for Afghanistan surged back, and he tried to share that with Tony.

But when Tony had to go, Kyle was left in the room on his own. And the self-doubts assailed him. Was that all he was good for now, storytelling?

It wasn't enough. With a pang of frustration he realized this afternoon had served one good purpose. It had shown him more clearly than ever before that he was fooling himself to cling to Sara's assurance that he could resurrect some kind of life in this place.

By listening to her, he'd clung to hope like a crutch. But today the crutch had been wrenched away when he'd embarrassed himself by showing the entire town that he could no longer even stand on his own. Surely Sara would have to admit that. There was no way he could forge a future here.

Look at me. I was totally dependent on Sara to

get me out of there. Now I have to wait for Teddy to get me home.

"No," he said out loud. "I will not live like that, dependent on others, no matter what anyone says, not even Sara."

But as he said it, Kyle suddenly realized the gap there would be in his life, a gap only Sara could fill.

And that scared him more than anything the military had put him through.

Chapter Eight

"I can't thank you all enough," Laurel said as she scanned each firelit face. "Without you, I don't know if we could have done it."

"To Laurel and her very successful grand opening," Sara said, lifting her glass of punch. She leaned over and clinked the rim against Kyle's. "Today was a total success."

"Hear, hear," Teddy said. "I don't know how you came up with the idea, but it was a great one."

"Sara might not think so tomorrow," Laurel said, brushing aside his compliment. "That crowd almost ate us out of house and home."

"Close." Sara chuckled as a rush of pride filled her. "There are only four tarts, two pieces of fudge and three pieces of pie left over."

"Anyone like another hot dog before we move on to what's left of dessert?" Teddy asked. When the others groaned and patted their stomachs, he grinned. "I guess I'll just have to eat this one my-self then," he said.

"I love campfires," Tony said. "Kyle knows lots of good stories. We could make them into camp-fire stories."

"What makes a campfire story?" Sara felt a rush of heat rise up her neck to her face as boys and adults alike turned to stare at her. Determined not to show how embarrassed she was that she couldn't share such a simple thing, she shrugged. "I lived in the city. We never had campfires."

"I don't suppose a lot of city kids do get to sit around a fire anymore," Kyle said thoughtfully. "I suppose you'll count this fire as another of those blessings you're always talking about."

"Depends on your story," she shot back with a wink. Immediately she felt self-conscious. Was it being too familiar to wink at a man?

But Kyle only grinned at her, so she relaxed.

After hearing Tony extoll Kyle's virtues as a storyteller, everyone was eager to hear him tell more about the North, this place they now called home.

Good, Sara thought. *That's exactly what I want. If Kyle can dig up happy memories of the past, maybe he'll finally let go of some of his sorrow.*

"What kind of story are you going to tell us, Kyle?" she asked.

"Me?" Kyle glared at her. "Why not Teddy?"

"I'm not a true northerner," Teddy protested. "I'm

just a visitor who loves this place and keeps coming back. You have more experiences in your little finger than I'll ever know. Why not share some?"

"About what?" Kyle frowned.

"About polar bears," Sara said before anyone else could suggest a topic. "Lucy told me one was hauled off to polar bear jail yesterday, though I'm not sure exactly what that is. Can you tell us, Kyle?"

The other boys chimed in on the question. Everyone looked toward Kyle for an explanation. He turned his head to shoot Sara a look she interpreted to mean he'd have preferred to remain silent. Eventually he gave a resigned sigh and explained.

"The jail is a building in a compound on the outskirts of the town. It's divided into cells in which they put bears who have roamed too close to town." Kyle stopped as if he'd finished explaining, but the boys wouldn't let him get away with such a meager explanation.

"Come on, Kyle," Tony said.

"Yeah, tell us more than that," another insisted.

"Guess we won't have to worry about a visit from a bear tonight," Kyle said with a grin. "It's too noisy. All right." He held up his hands. "It's a specially designed jail. The goal is to keep the bears isolated from human contact and reintroduce them back into the wild, but away from Churchill. The wildlife service doesn't want to hurt them, but it does want to protect both those who live here and the bears that pass through and use the Hudson Bay to migrate."

"Migrate to where?" Rod seemed totally enthralled.

"You want their migration schedule? This is going to take a while," Kyle muttered.

"We're not going anywhere," one of the boys said. Then he grinned. "Because there's nowhere to go."

Sara hid her smile as the boys burst into laughter at the joke. She was delighted the kids weren't allowing Kyle to stop. She fell under the spell of his words when he related the bear's phases from the birth of a cub to its journey to adulthood.

She could listen to him forever.

By the time Kyle finished, Sara was certain each boy would soon be on the internet, searching for more information on polar bears. She had a hunch they would have tried tonight but Laurel insisted it was too late and they'd have to wait till tomorrow.

The newly informed boys willingly lugged dishes and carefully stored their refuse, conscious now that they must not leave anything that would attract wildlife. They now wanted to be part of the bears' protection. Sara whispered a prayer of thanksgiving as she loaded the dishwasher and cleaned the counters.

She startled when she noticed Kyle standing in the shadows and automatically checked his eyes to gauge whether he was in pain. But his expression was closed and she couldn't tell. So she asked, "Anything wrong?"

"Nothing except that I can't leave. Teddy's in Laurel's office showing her some computer accounting program he brought her, so I can't go home yet."

"At least they're not arguing about something. That seems like progress, don't you think?"

He shared her smile. "Maybe a little. But I need to get home."

"Why?" She chuckled. He was so easy to talk to, and so much fun to tease. "You don't have a curfew, do you?"

"No." A glimmer of a smile tugged at his lips. He leaned one hip against the chair rail that projected halfway up the wall.

Sara couldn't help admiring him. He was so handsome, so…in control.

"I'd planned to help Rod with graphics for his web page this evening, but I guess that will have to wait for another day." He studied her. "How's the search for your mom going?"

After a moment, Sara said, "I did find something I wanted to ask you about."

She'd debated whether to bother Kyle again. Not that her questions seemed to irritate him. He'd been patient and understanding. But after that confrontation in his living room, Sara felt she was taking too much of his time.

"Well, I'm here now." He waited. "Go ahead and ask."

"It would be easier to explain if I showed you. Would you mind taking a look?"

There was a trace of hesitation before he said, "Sure."

"Thanks. I appreciate it." Sara led the way to the computer room, glad that the boys weren't there. She needed for this to be private.

Once the computer had booted up, she clicked on the site she'd previously saved. "I'm not sure what this message means."

"It's just someone trying to sell something. It's nothing." His hand covered hers on the mouse as he clicked it. Sara gasped at the contact, hoping he didn't notice how flustered she was. A new page was now visible.

Kyle leaned over her shoulder to read the screen. He caught his breath. "Sara, this is from eight years ago. Maybe you shouldn't—"

"What?" She turned her head. His face was mere inches from hers and her heart raced.

"Nothing." His face closed up.

"It's about a tornado in Ontario," she said, turning back to read the screen. "My mother's name led me here so there must be something about her, but it keeps changing so I can't get where I want to go. See?"

"Let me sit there for a minute, would you?"

Sara traded places with Kyle, admiring the way his capable hands flew over the keys while she waited. Part of her wanted to read whatever it had to say about her mother, but another part, a part she kept pushing away, was afraid to read it.

She'd told herself she'd been too busy getting ready for the grand opening, that she hadn't had the time or energy to get back on this site. But her need to find her mother outweighed that tiny fear crouched deep inside. Maybe her mother had moved to Ontario. Maybe there was information about her new address. Maybe she'd finally find her mother and the rest of her family.

Hope built fast and furious until her brain urged *Hurry. Hurry. Hurry, Kyle.*

"Okay." Kyle rose and stepped to one side, his voice devoid of all emotion. "Click on it again," he told her.

"But what if—"

"Are you afraid to see what's there?" he demanded.

"Yes. A little," she admitted. "But I still want to know." She frowned at him. "I want to know the truth, whatever it is."

"Then click on it," Kyle ordered.

Not understanding why he sounded so harsh, Sara clicked the mouse and watched the page refresh.

"I don't see my mother's name or anything about her on here," she said. "In fact, this isn't quite the same. It looks like some kind of newspaper article now."

"It is. The *Scarborough Tribune*. Scroll down. You may find something near the bottom." Again he sounded angry and she didn't know why.

After a sideways glance at his face, Sara could feel tension grip Kyle's body. She saw his fist clench against his thigh as if to prepare for something. She wanted to ask him what was wrong but didn't. It had been a long day. Maybe his leg hurt?

"What are you waiting for, Sara?"

"Oh, sorry. I'm holding you up, aren't I?" She scrolled down, scanning paragraphs for the name she wanted. At the bottom of the page she saw it. Eagerly she read the information under the heading "Twister."

And stopped.

"Oh, please, God, no." Her breath snagged in her throat. Her heart beat like a lead mallet in her chest. Hot tears rolled down her face and Sara was utterly powerless to stop them.

Among the dead was a forty-nine-year-old woman, Sophia Kane, believed to be traveling through the area when the tornado struck. Next of kin have yet to be notified.

"Sara." Kyle's fingers closed around her shoulders, turning her face away from the computer screen so she could see only him. "I'm so sorry."

"She's dead, Kyle. All this time I've been dreaming about how we'd connect and how she'd tell me she'd always loved me and wanted me back and—she's dead?" She looked at him, silently begging him to make it better and knowing he couldn't. No one could. "Why didn't I know? Why didn't I feel it? Shouldn't you know when your own mother dies? Shouldn't there be a bond that's broken and you know they're gone?"

"I didn't know when my dad died," he murmured. "I was closer to him than you were to your mom and I didn't know, so don't feel guilty." His arms drew her up. He rose with her and held her close, pressing her against him.

"I feel—stupid, like I should have known," she sobbed.

"How could you know?" Kyle's fingers threaded through her hair, smoothing back the strands. Though he wiped the tears from her cheeks repeatedly, more kept coming.

Desperate to feel connected to someone, Sara slid her arms around Kyle's neck and hung on as a storm of grief battered her heart.

Nothing in her world felt secure anymore. Nothing but Kyle.

What would she do when he left?

And yet he wasn't really hers to hang on to. What man would ever want someone like her, someone without a base, a heritage, even a history? Someone who didn't know anything about loving or being loved?

No man would want a woman like her. But for now, for a few moments, she clung to Kyle as the knowledge that she'd never hear her mother's voice again, never see her face or feel her love, swamped her.

"I know how much it hurts, Sara." His breath grazed the tip of her ear as he whispered the words. "I only wish I could make it better for you."

"You are." She tucked her head under his chin, wondering how she'd go on, alone. "Thank you for being here, Kyle."

If only he could stay, be the one she could turn to. Always.

In sudden clarity, Sara knew her feelings for this man were changing, but to what? She was confused by the crazy joy that exploded inside when he held her. She had to distance herself. Now.

Accepting the tissue Kyle pressed into her hands, she gently pulled away from him.

"I'm sorry for soaking your shirt," she murmured.

"My shirt doesn't matter." He pressed the damp strands of hair back from her face. "What will you do now, Sara?"

"Do?" She frowned at him. "I'll keep looking for clues, of course. I still haven't found my father."

Kyle seemed astonished. "You want to go on searching?"

"If it was your family, wouldn't you?" she demanded.

"Maybe not right after I'd received this news," he said. "You're one gutsy lady, Sara Kane."

"The way you say it, I'm not sure if that's a good thing or a bad thing," she said, forcing a laugh but unable to dismiss the respect in his words.

Kyle's stare made Sara uncomfortable. If she wasn't so clueless about men, she might have thought that was admiration glimmering in his eyes. But why would Kyle admire her? She'd never been anywhere or done anything special. She wasn't a hero like him.

"I meant is as a compliment, Sara." Said like that, she couldn't doubt his sincerity.

"Well, thank you." She blushed and backed away. The look in his eyes made her stomach flutter nervously. What was wrong with her? "I guess Teddy is probably looking for you. You must want to get home. Is your leg giving you pain?"

For some reason that question seemed to irritate him. "My leg is fine," he said.

"Good." She didn't know what else to say.

"Can I ask you something, Sara?"

Surprised, she nodded.

"What do you think about Rod's website idea?"

The question surprised her. She stared at him, watching as he leaned back on his heels. But he was watching her, his gaze unsettling as he watched her print off the page about her mother then shut down the computer.

"It seems to help him accept his uncle's death. Maybe it would help others if they could get online and talk to someone who's gone through what they have." She tilted her head to look at him. "Did you find it helpful to share your sorrow over your mother's death?"

"I didn't talk to anyone. Why do people always assume you'll feel better if you talk?" he demanded in a cranky tone.

"Because a sorrow shared is a sorrow beared, or something like that." She frowned. "I can't remember exactly how Lucy put it but it made sense at the time."

A laugh burst from him.

"What's so funny?" She walked to the door and waited for him to catch up.

"You're just like Lucy. For as long as I can remember she's always tried to ease someone else's load, too. It's—admirable," he said after a tiny pause.

"The Bible says we're supposed to share one another's burdens," she reminded him.

"I knew you'd say that." Kyle's broad shoulders shook with laughter again. He stopped in front of her and tilted her chin up so he could look into her eyes. His own sparkled with amusement.

"Are you laughing at me?" she said, feeling foolish and sort of offended at the same time.

"Admiring you," Kyle corrected. "If there's one thing I can count on with you, Sara, it's that you will always, somehow, someway, bring the discussion back to God."

"Don't you think God's worth thinking about?" She didn't expect him to answer. Kyle had become an expert at dodging her questions whenever he didn't want to reveal his thoughts.

Sara said nothing as she led him to the kitchen and poured them both a glass of juice and set them on the table.

"I do think about God, Sara." Kyle's voice emerged in a low whisper. "I think about Him a lot. I think about what He was doing when my parents died and when I lost my leg. Where was He when your mother died?" His eyes burned into her.

Sara held his gaze, silently praying for words that would help him shed his anger, words that would lift him up and enable him to see possibilities. She could hear Teddy and Laurel arguing as they came down the hall, and knew she had only a second or two before they arrived. So she said the only thing she could think of.

"I can't be angry at God," she murmured. "He has a plan for my life. I just don't know what it is yet."

It hurt to see pity fill Kyle's face. Sara didn't know what to say, how to make him understand, so she said nothing. Soon after that the men left and Laurel went to bed, leaving Sara alone.

She wandered into the living room and sank down on the floor in front of the huge picture window that looked out across the tundra.

The full moon lit the world in front of her so brightly it looked like early morning. As a hush descended on the building, Sara thought back on her conversation with Kyle. How she longed for him to let go of his pain and renew his faith.

"Show me how to help him, Lord. Make me a blessing."

As she prayed, she couldn't stop replaying those moments in the computer room with him. His comforting embrace had soothed the pain of her mother's loss but it had also reenergized her yearning to be loved.

"Kyle needs Your help, God. He's getting himself tied up in anger and loss and losing sight of all You've given him."

As usual, thoughts of Kyle made her heart race. Just being near him brought all sorts of odd reactions she'd never felt before. She hardly dared think it, but could this be love?

Sara didn't know. Anything she knew about love came from the books she'd read. But these feelings inside her weren't like anything she'd read about. What was love, anyway?

It was affection, fondness for another hurting soul. She certainly felt all of that for Kyle. He was her friend, so of course she cared about him.

She pulled Laurel's Bible near and turned to 1 Corinthians 13. Carefully with great thought, she read the entire passage.

"That's it exactly," she whispered in wonderment. Her fingers traced the words again.

If you love someone, you will be loyal to him no matter what the cost. You will always believe in him, always expect the best of him, and always stand your ground in defending him.

The words felt right and true when applied to what was inside her heart.

"So do I love Kyle, God? And if I do, what do I do about it?"

Across town, in the darkness of his family home, Kyle couldn't settle. He knew his unease had to do with Sara. That unsettled him even more.

She was utterly beautiful, inside and out. She loved reaching out to everyone, spreading compassion on everyone. There seemed no end to her pluck and Kyle was embarrassed by his growing need to know how this delicate woman, who had grown up in the difficult world of foster care, had acquired her tender heart.

Ask her, his brain ordered. Guilt rushed over him as he remembered the many times he'd rebuffed her questions. He hadn't been willing to share his past with her. How could he now pry into hers?

The laptop sat in the corner, waiting to answer his questions with a few keystrokes. Kyle knew exactly how to coax answers from it in a very short space of time. And yet…

Part of him rebelled at such a blatant invasion of her privacy. The other part argued that if he knew what made her the way she was, maybe he'd be able to show her that dependence on God was not going to help her.

Finally, he opened the laptop, booted it up and initiated his search.

Ten minutes later Kyle was reeling, stunned by the depravity of foster parents who'd kept Sara imprisoned as their personal slave, preying on her neediness and innocence for years. The ugly details filled him with anger, shock and a thousand questions. Why had she stayed, and how had enduring such horror left Sara with her deep and abiding inner joy and faith in God?

He shut down the computer. Tomorrow he'd ask her.

Kyle tossed that idea away as quickly as it had come. If he asked Sara why she was so positive God was on her side after she'd suffered so much, she'd know he'd been prying into her life. She'd also sing

God's praises to him yet again, and he did not want to hear that. Bitterness welled up inside at the betrayal of faith he and Sara had both suffered.

But Sara doesn't feel betrayed, an inner voice whispered.

He wanted—no, needed—to help her. Why not go to Lives more often? He could say Rod wanted help with his website or ask Tony, the would-be mechanic, to help rebuild his old ATV. Whatever the excuse, Kyle would talk to Sara and find a way to help her.

The message light flashed on the phone. Kyle pushed the button. Elation rushed in when the Realtor asked to show the house.

Except, if it sold right away, he'd never find out how Sara—

"First you have to get the offer," he said aloud. "And when you do, Sara and Lives Under Construction cannot come into it. You aren't staying here. You're leaving."

Funny how saying that aloud cast a pall over him.

Kyle hobbled to his room. Amazingly, he hadn't taken a pain pill all day. Not even after he'd fallen flat in front of the entire town, which didn't seem so terrible now. In fact, his public humiliation lost all significance when he compared it to Sara's miserable childhood and the added indignity of having that ugliness repeated in the tabloids during the court case.

All Kyle had to do was watch his step, but Sara—how could she get over the things she'd gone through? She hoped finding her family would heal her past but Kyle wasn't so sure.

The memory of her sobbing against his shoulder made him feel helpless.

If only he could—

No! He needed to forget about the tenderness Sara roused in his heart. He had to erase memories of that tickle of delight that shimmied down his arm when his hand brushed her hair. He must obliterate the rush of joy he felt when she laughed. Sleep vanished as he remembered every heart-stirring detail of the day with her.

She can't be more than a friend, his brain reminded.

Nothing more.

Kyle's last thoughts before he finally found sleep were of silver-gray eyes and the sound of gently amused laughter.

A beautiful face, and an even more beautiful heart.

Chapter Nine

On June 21, Sara went to the beach after dinner.

Since it was the longest day of the year she intended to stay awhile—daylight now lasted well into the wee morning hours. She sat on a bench, backed by the massive, smooth boulders that surrounded Hudson Bay, mesmerized by the elegant dips and dives of gigantic whales floating in the bay.

Silently she pleaded with God to lead her to her father.

"Sara?"

She turned her head. Kyle stood several feet away, breathing heavily from the effort of making his way out to her.

"May I join you?"

"Sure." She studied his careful progress toward her, noting how he avoided the lichen-covered bits of rock, which might be slippery.

"What are you doing?" he asked.

"Enjoying this." She moved her arm to include the panorama before them. "It's nine o'clock at night yet still as bright as this morning. I can't get over it."

"All part of living in the North," he said with a grin. "And you're not the only one enjoying the light." He pointed out the lawn chairs dotting the crest of the hill above them. "When summer arrives in Churchill, we don't like to miss a day."

She smiled at the *we*. So he still considered himself a Native. Good. Maybe he'd finally realize how much he was needed here.

Kyle sat beside her, his shoulder brushing hers. Unnerved by his touch, Sara turned her attention back to the bay and pointed.

"See those whales? They're black. But I read that Churchill whales are white."

"There are two main types of whales that come here," he explained. "Beluga whales are a gray-white. They go into the Churchill river to have their babies." He pointed. "They come right alongside a boat, so close you can pet their heads."

"Really?" She sighed. "I would love to do that."

"I used to do it in a kayak," he murmured, his gaze on the horizon, deep in thought. After a moment he spoke again. "Those—" he pointed toward the bay "—are the big guys. They also come here to give birth but because of their size, they have to stay in the bay where the water's deeper."

"Laurel said something about there being a fort

here?" She leaned back, thrilling to the sound of his deep voice and the way his whole manner grew more animated when he spoke about the town.

"Of course. Prince of Wales Fort," Kyle told her. "Originally called Eskimo Point. Dad and I used to do a boat tour there.

"The fort was built by the Hudson's Bay Company in 1717 to protect and control their interests in the fur trade. It has forty-two cannons with more across the river at Cape Merry. It's a protected heritage site now."

Sara hugged her arms around her waist and imagined Churchill long ago. "This place has so much history. Everywhere you look there's evidence of people pulling together, of families building their homes in a new and unfamiliar land. I'm going to miss the community's closeness when I leave at Christmas."

"What's stopping you from staying?" he asked, one eyebrow arched.

"I took Laurel's job for six months to give me time to make some decisions about my future. I'm kind of like you, Kyle." She smiled at him, but because looking at him made her catch her breath, she refocused on the bay. "Churchill is a great place to get away from—everything."

"I guess."

"But I can't stay here, much as I love it. I need to

figure out what God has planned for me in the world and get busy at it."

"You can't do whatever it is here?" His voice held unasked questions.

How could she explain her belief that she needed to learn how to fit in with people, how to function on her own without Laurel or anyone else's support? She couldn't say that.

"I can't stay without a job and that ends at Christmas." She smiled at his puzzled look. "Laurel was my social worker but she's become a sort of mother to me. I had an isolated childhood. She agrees that I need to go back to the city where I used to live and rebuild my life."

"But surely if you wanted to stay—"

"If it was part of God's plan for me, I would, but I believe staying here would be too easy. It's too comfortable for me here. I wouldn't have to change and grow as much." She struggled to explain what she meant. "I need to change who I am and how I see the world."

"I don't think you need to change anything. I think you'll fit in perfectly well wherever you go."

"Thank you." Flustered by his compliment, she kept her gaze forward. It would be hard to leave Lives, but especially hard to leave Kyle. "Besides, Laurel's already recruiting someone to take my place."

"Maybe she thinks there aren't enough single

men here." He eased his leg into a more comfortable position.

"Why would that matter?" Sara asked in confusion.

"Well, if she's concerned about your future, she probably wants you to meet somebody, fall in love, get married and have kids."

Rattled by his searching glance, Sara blushed.

"You don't want to get married and have a family?" A sharp edge to his question made her look at him.

"I'd like that more than anything," she told him. "But I doubt it will happen."

"Why not?"

"Because…" It felt funny to be discussing this with Kyle. But he was sitting there, waiting for an answer, and she couldn't lie. "I'm not the kind of person men want to marry."

"You're not?" His eyes did a head-to-toe scan of her. "Why?"

"I'm a misfit." Sara avoided his eyes. "I'm not really good at anything important."

"I doubt the kids would say that come breakfast time." His eyes crinkled when he smiled.

"Anybody can cook." She shrugged that off.

"I can't." He kept his gaze on her. "Why else wouldn't someone want to marry you?"

"I'm not pretty," she admitted, embarrassed by his continued probing. "I'm not normal. I don't know anything about fashion or how to dress. I certainly don't know anything about love or, uh, romance. I've never even dated."

Kyle was silent for a long time. Sara could feel the intensity of his stare cutting across any pretense she might have offered. So she sat silent, embarrassed and ashamed.

"Sara, not every man is concerned about glamour or looks. Not that you have to worry. You're a very beautiful woman." He touched her arm as if to reinforce his words.

"You don't have to say that," she whispered. "I know I'm not pretty."

"Have you looked in a mirror recently?" He barked out a laugh. "Your eyes are amazing. Your face could be on a magazine. On top of all that you're an awesome cook." His voice lowered to a serious tone. "But what matters most is that you have a generous, tender heart that cares for people. That's the most attractive thing about you. Caring for people is what you do best. It's why the boys care about you so much."

"Thank you for saying that, Kyle," she whispered, more embarrassed than ever by his fulsome praise. "It's very kind of you."

"I'm not being kind." His loud voice drew the attention of some passersby. "Listen to me, Sara. I got myself engaged to a woman who was all of the things you think are so important. But when I lost my leg, she took off without even saying goodbye. She was disgusted by me."

The pain darkening Kyle's eyes made Sara long to hug him, but before she could console him, he continued.

"You have more beauty in your little finger than she had in her whole body, Ms. Kane. And whatever you say, I think you know more about love than most people."

Kyle thought she knew about love? Inside her heart the persistent flicker of admiration she always felt for him flared into a full-fledged flame. But Sara didn't know how to respond. If she wasn't careful, his kindness would coax her into confessing the ugliness of her past and then he'd see that she wasn't any of those things he'd said.

"You don't believe me," he said in a flat tone.

She smiled at him then turned to gaze over the water and said, "You said you used to kayak. Can't you do that anymore?"

"No." No room for explanation there.

"How do you know?" She didn't flinch under his glare. "I just wonder how you can be so sure you can't do it if you haven't tried. Did you sell your kayak?"

"No. But I intend to." His jaw thrust out as he stared straight ahead. "The past is over, Sara."

"Perhaps. But it seems to me that you're giving up too easily on the future." She knew he didn't want to hear that, but he didn't say anything so she kept speaking. "I read about Zodiacs. Maybe you could use one of those. What is it, anyway?"

"A kind of inflated boat," he said with a frown.

"I saw this in the grocery store." She pulled a pamphlet from her pocket. "It's a Zodiac ride to see the belugas. I'm going to do that as soon as I save up enough money."

"You'll have to do it before fall," he told her. "They migrate south and the river freezes."

"Then I will," she assured him. "I am going to do that."

They sat shoulder to shoulder in a companionable silence for a long time.

"I should get going." Sara loathed ending the time she'd spent with Kyle. She'd never had a friend to talk to like this, but tomorrow morning would come early and for as long as she was here, she had no intention of shirking her job. She hesitated to offer her help, wondering if Kyle felt less manly when she did. "How did you get here?" she asked instead.

"I wondered when you'd ask." Kyle's eyes sparkled. "I have transport. Over there." He pointed and she saw a giant yellow machine. "It's my old ATV. Tony helped me get it running. Now I can get around on my own." His face changed. "At least until the snow flies. Or until I sell the house."

"Will that happen soon?" She couldn't help the flutter of worry that Kyle would leave before he realized he still had a lot to give to Churchill, before he realized he didn't have to leave here to have a future.

Or was she worrying that he would leave before she did?

"I've had two showings but so far no sale." He walked beside her across the beach. "Two more days and school will be out for the summer. Then what will the boys do?"

"They'll have summer school, but I don't know what else Laurel has planned." Sara pushed her bicycle toward Kyle's ATV. "She wants to teach them more about Churchill but she hasn't been here long enough to really know the history."

"They can see Canada Day celebrated in true Churchillian style on the first of July." Kyle leaned one hip against his machine. "They'll learn a lot about this place from that."

"Are there fireworks?"

"We don't have fireworks in summer. It's too bright at night. We save them for New Year's Eve." He grinned as if he remembered happier times. Then his face changed. "Any news about your dad, Sara?"

"No." Sara tried to hide her worry. "I found a couple of sites but I think they refer to someone else with the same name."

Why can't I find him, Lord? Don't You want me to have a family to love?

Over and over Sara had reassured herself with Scripture that God is a God of love, that He wants the best for His children. But in spite of that, doubt had begun to root.

She glanced at Kyle's house and thought again of the sweet family he'd been given, of the love that had filled his home and his youth. Why couldn't she have that?

"I could take a look now," Kyle offered. "If you want."

"I'd like that." She had to duck her head to hide her delight at spending more time with Kyle.

"Let's go." His grin made his scar less noticeable. At Kyle's nod Sara began pedaling up the gravelly incline and onto the street. She rode back to Lives, conscious of the sputtering motor behind her.

When they pulled into the yard, the boys ended their basketball game and crowded around Kyle's machine, inundating him with questions.

"One at a time." He made a point of telling the boys to ask Tony their questions, since he was the one who'd helped him fix the ATV.

As Sara watched the proud boy stretch taller, a tiny thrill rushed through her. Kyle's generosity proved he was a man who cared, whether or not he acknowledged it.

"Got anything for snacks, Sara?" the oldest boy, Barry, asked. "We're starving."

"As usual." She grinned. "I made fresh dough-nuts this afternoon. I hid them in the oven. Help yourself." She looked at Kyle. "I suppose you want some, too?"

"Fresh doughnuts?" He nodded vigorously. "I definitely want some."

"Hot chocolate and doughnuts," Sara confirmed. "Let's go." She hurried inside, prepared the cocoa then sat at the table, relishing the laughter and teasing. This was what she longed for—her own home, her own family.

Finished, the boys thanked her, cleaned up then headed to their rooms. Kyle had disappeared, too, but when she carried her mug of tea into the computer room, she found him studying Rod's website.

"What do you think of it?" she asked.

"He's getting a ton of hits. Apparently a lot of servicemen and women want to talk about what they endured over there. I didn't expect that. Most of the guys I worked with kept it inside."

"Like you?" She smiled when he frowned at her. "But that doesn't help."

"Do you know a lot about keeping ugliness inside?" he asked, blue eyes darkening.

"I know something about it. I—I didn't have a very good childhood, Kyle, but the memories got easier when I spoke to my pastor about it. He helped me understand that I'm not a victim, I am a survivor. That's been important to me in letting go of the past."

"That's why you're always talking about how good God is?"

"Sort of." There was an intensity in Kyle's tone that told Sara this was an important moment, so she said a prayer for words to help him understand.

"There wasn't much goodness where I grew up. I watched as the kids who lived with me ached for someone to love them, someone to tell them it was going to be okay."

"I have a feeling you did that for them," he said thoughtfully.

"If I could." Sara leaned forward. "The thing is, everybody goes through stuff, Kyle. Maybe they don't have abusive foster parents like me, or lose a limb as you have, but everyone has something they have to deal with. If we don't face it, it will forever color our future, so I try to face it every day. When I do, I grow stronger."

"I guess you were right."

"I was?" She blinked.

"You keep saying people feel better after talking to someone about their issues." He waved at the screen. "These folks do seem to find relief in sharing. Some of the things I've read on Rod's site—" Kyle shook his head. "I feel ashamed that I've bellyached so much about my lot."

"The point isn't who's suffered more." She touched his arm and looked straight into his eyes. "What's so great about Rod's site is that it allows each of you to see that you're not alone, that others suffered and that there are people who care that you were willing to sacrifice for your country. That's how God is. He never leaves us alone."

To her surprise, Kyle didn't argue. He stared into her eyes for several moments as if he was thinking about what she'd said.

For Sara, that connection went right to that secret place inside where she hid her feelings. Afraid that Kyle would see just how much she'd begun to care what he thought of her, she focused on the computer.

"So this is what I've found about my dad. It must be someone else with the same name." She frowned when he made no response. As he studied the page, his brows drew together. She moved the cursor to change pages.

"Wait." He put his hand on hers and guided the mouse to a line before clicking. A list of names appeared. "Is this birth date right?"

"Yes, but I can't get it to reveal anything else. What am I doing wrong?"

"Wait a minute." He put his hand over hers on the mouse and pressed. The screen changed. "Try again."

She did and her father's name appeared in the center of the screen. A frisson of hope flickered inside until she noticed something. "Kyle, this is a list of obituaries, isn't it?"

"Let me see." He leaned closer, studied the screen then looked at her, sadness filling his eyes. "Yes."

"This is dated eleven years ago." She couldn't believe it. "He's dead. My father is dead?" All this time, all the searching, for nothing? She peered at the page. "He died when I was eleven," she whispered.

"I'm sorry." Kyle stared at her. "Are you all right?"

"I don't know." Sara struggled to express what was going on inside. "I don't really have any strong memories of him. A feeling of being carried, a vague image of his face, that's all." She caught her breath. "But I never thought, I never imagined—" Tears spilled from her eyes and tumbled down her cheeks. "I'm an orphan," she whispered.

"Sara, please don't cry." Kyle's arms went around her and he drew her against his shoulder. "You have friends here," he whispered. His fingers threaded through her hair as he spoke, his soft, gentle tone matching the cadence of his words. "You have people who love you, Sara, who care about you. You're not alone."

"Yes, I am." She drew away from him, dashed her knuckles across her eyes and let the full weight of this new knowledge impact her heart. "I have no mother, no father. No one." The words whispered from her in a wrenching sob.

"Neither do I."

Kyle's stark response stunned Sara. She looked

into his deep blue eyes. In that moment she understood the sense of total aloneness Kyle had been dealing with ever since he'd stepped off the train.

How could she have so cavalierly insisted he get on with his life? Compassion rose up in a wave and she leaned forward and wrapped her arms around him.

"I'm sorry, Kyle. I'm really sorry."

"You're sorry for me?" He sat frozen for a moment before he lifted his hands, slid them around her waist and drew her close. "Thank you." His breath brushed the tip of her ear.

She marveled at the strength of his arms around her, at the security she felt.

"It's like you can't wake up from a dream. You don't know where to turn, what to do next. It feels so…" She paused. "Empty."

Kyle said nothing, simply hugged her closer. His lips brushed over her cheek.

No man had ever kissed her like that before. An explosion of emotion rose inside, feelings of wonderment, sweet and tender. An emotion akin to reverence swept over her when he finally drew away.

"It must be doubly hard for you," she realized aloud. "I didn't really know my father. I can't imagine how you deal with being here, seeing and touching all the things your dad loved. I didn't consider that. I'm sorry."

"Don't be sad for me, Sara." Kyle leaned back,

using the pad of one thumb to erase the tear marks from beneath her eyes. "Anyway, you're not alone, like me. Aren't you always telling me you have God to bless you?"

"Yes." Sara frowned. "But you're not alone, either, Kyle. You have the entire community just waiting to support you."

There was a long pause while he studied her. Then he leaned forward and kissed her cheek.

As she followed him to the door and waved good-night, a voice in the back of her mind whispered, *You have me, Kyle. I'm here and I care about you.*

After he'd driven away and she was left alone, staring at the half-lit sky, Sara touched her cheek. This was love; she was certain of it. The tenderness that was flickering to life inside her had to be the real thing. For the first time in her life she felt she was important to someone, to Kyle.

Did he need her as much as she needed him? She wondered if being Kyle's friend would salve the ache in her heart to be loved.

Chapter Ten

Kyle's revelation started on Canada Day, when it seemed everyone he spoke to knew or had been inspired by Sara Kane.

"Sara made the Canada Day cake."

"Sara's put together a treasure hunt for the little kids."

In the days that followed, songs of Sara's generosity filled his ears every time he stepped out of the house. Everyone in town knew Sara.

"The talent show is Sara Kane's doing," an old friend told him.

"She encouraged town council to arrange it," the mayor confided. "We couldn't get anyone to participate until some of the boys from Lives agreed to take part to raise money for our new fire hall."

Someone came by to donate more soil for "Sara's plants." A local business offered to repair Laurel's ratty van for "Sara's boys." Even town council had chimed in, promising that come fall, transportation would be provided for "Sara's kids," thus freeing Laurel from four daily trips into town.

Kyle found rich irony in realizing Sara had even drawn *him* into the summer activities at Lives, though he'd intended to remain detached. The box kites he'd helped the boys build, the ones they were now flying, were her idea.

"I always wanted to fly a kite," she'd said. And somehow Kyle just had to make that dream come true.

Now as Kyle watched Rod show Sara how to turn her brilliant yellow kite out over the cliffs, he found he couldn't look away. Her eyes flashed, her cheeks bloomed and her hair streamed behind her in carefree abandon. She gave a whoop of joyful triumph as she leaned into the wind and let the kite soar. Kyle thought he could watch her forever and that bothered him.

He was getting too fond of Sara Kane. After today he'd have to work harder on keeping his distance.

"This was a great idea," Sara said. Having handed the kite to Rod, she flopped onto their blanket on a sun-warmed rock. "It's a perfect day. Look at the boys. They're having so much fun. *I* had so much fun."

"I'm glad." Kyle lowered himself awkwardly beside her. "But I'm not sure I can do much more of this," he said sotto voce, aware that the boys were mere feet away reeling in their kite string. "I'm not good on this kind of terrain."

"I realize you've put yourself out to do this with us," she said. "I wouldn't have had a clue how to teach them to fly a kite. I appreciate your help."

"My pleasure." And it was.

Kyle enjoyed every encounter with her. But more than that, he now realized that as much as Sara and Laurel tried to make Lives as homey as possible, the boys were missing out on the maturing experiences his father had provided to enrich his own life, experiences that required a male perspective. He wasn't the right man to do that for them. But until someone else came along, who else was there?

Of course, being around Sara was no hardship.

"What's the worst part?" she asked.

"I can manage the beach, pretty much," he qualified. "But these rocks are something else."

"I've been praying for you, Kyle." Sara smiled and placed her hand over his. "And I believe God will help you do whatever you set your mind to."

"I hope so." For once he wasn't going to argue. When she removed her hand from his, some of the warmth drained out of the day. "I don't want to make a spectacle of myself."

"Would it matter so much?" Her stare was intense.

"To me, yes."

"I read a verse this morning. 'Happy is he whose hope is in the Lord his God, which made heaven and earth, the sea, and all that therein is: which keepeth truth forever.' It's from Psalms 146." Her silver-gray eyes shone with confidence. "God didn't abandon you, Kyle. I'm more certain of that than ever. He has plans for your life. You just have to keep your hope focused on God."

While Kyle studied Sara's face, a tiny part of his hardened heart melted. But he couldn't afford to get soft, certainly not about Sara, who so desperately wanted a family.

He couldn't give that to her, even if a relationship between them was possible.

And it wasn't. He was leaving Churchill. Soon.

Kyle turned away from her and stared across the bay. Tiny ripples toyed with the glassy surface. As usual, Sara's words challenged him.

In fact, it was the way she'd so quickly found solace in God after learning of her father's death that compelled him to seek out the new minister in town.

"You have an error in your thinking, Kyle." Rick Salinger hadn't used fancy phrases or tried to pretend that he was anything other than a young pastor in a small, isolated community.

"I do?"

"God doesn't leave us, not even when we try to push Him away. He stays and He waits for us until we're ready to hear what He has to say. No matter how long it takes. Because He loves us."

"Kyle?" Sara's hand on his arm roused him from this morning's early conversation.

"Yeah?" Kyle raised one eyebrow, surprised by the concern on her face. He thought about telling her of his visit to Rick this morning but changed his mind. For now he needed to think about it on his own for a while. "Sorry. What did you say?"

"Do you want to eat lunch now?"

Since the boys were trying to outdo each other in running their kites higher, he decided to use the opportunity to talk to her. "First I want to ask you something."

"Okay." She stopped lifting dishes out of the basket, folded her hands in her lap and waited.

"What will you do about your family now that you know your parents are…gone?" He hesitated to say it, not wanting to hurt her.

"I'm not sure." Now she was the one who stared across the bay. "The thing is, Kyle, I think I might have a brother."

"What?" He blinked at her statement. "You *think?*"

"I know it sounds odd. Listen, and I'll try to explain. For many years I've had nightmares about a child crying and calling for me. At least I thought it was a nightmare." Her hands clenched.

"I'm listening, Sara," Kyle encouraged.

"I was almost thirteen when I was taken to the Masters' home to live. I had been in other foster homes by then, but none were as bad as the Masters'." She gulped. "It got worse the longer I was there. I guess somewhere along the way I blanked out my past."

Her face lost all life, all sparkle. It seemed to Kyle that the light he'd seen shining from inside her earlier had been snuffed out. She inhaled, peering straight ahead. Her voice emerged flat, emotionless.

"After six months, I made up my mind I wasn't going to stay."

"But how…" He felt confused.

"I decided to run away."

Kyle stayed silent, hoping she'd finally tell him about her past.

"It was bad." Sara clamped her lips together, clearly summoning all the courage she could find. "Anyway, I decided to leave. I waited until everyone was asleep, then I climbed out the kitchen window and ran. I made it two blocks."

Totally unnerved by the gray tone of her skin, Kyle wanted her to stop. But he knew Sara needed to get this story out.

Sara believed talking about things healed you. Kyle wanted her healed, so he wrapped an arm around her shoulder. She was shivering.

"Tell me the rest," he said softly as he draped his jacket over her shoulders.

"She followed me."

"Who followed you?" Shaken by the dead sound of her voice, Kyle grasped her icy fingers and held on.

"Maria." Sara hiccupped a sob and buried her face against his neck. "She was the sweetest four-year-old you've ever seen. She said I was her big sister." Her voice choked. Tears flowed down her pallid cheeks. "She died because she followed me. I didn't know it but I should have. She was always following me. I killed her."

"No, you didn't." Kyle saw the boys heading for them. They were frowning, clearly worried about Sara. He shook his head, grateful when they backed off. "You loved Maria as if she was your own baby sister." He knew it was true. Sara's big heart couldn't help but enfold a needy child.

"Yes, but—" She stopped.

"Tell me."

"She was running across the road to catch up, I think." She stopped again.

"All of it, Sara."

She inhaled. "I heard a thud, the sound of glass breaking and I heard her call my name. I couldn't figure out— I went back." Sara's hand on his tightened like a vise. "When I got there, Maria was lying in the street, her beautiful hair spread around her. She said she hurt and asked me to hold her. I didn't know if I should move her, but I couldn't just leave her like that."

"Of course you couldn't," Kyle agreed.

"I heard someone calling the police, but Maria kept begging me to hold her. So I cradled her head on my lap." Sara gulped. "She smiled and said thank-you before she drifted off. The ambulance was just arriving when she opened her eyes. She said didn't she make a good snow angel. And then she died."

"Oh, Sara." Kyle couldn't imagine any thirteen-year-old having to deal with such a tragedy. Clearly the guilt still clung. "I'd give anything to erase that memory from your mind." Kyle simply sat there, holding her as she wept.

"Maria died because of me and all anyone was worried about was these silly cuts." Sara's fingers rubbed the scars on her wrists as if she could erase them. "The worst thing was Maria died for nothing. I was too afraid to tell the police why I'd left so they made me go back to the Masters'. After that they locked me in the basement every night so I couldn't run away. They didn't need to do that. Believe me, I wasn't going anywhere."

Rage burned inside Kyle like an inferno. But he kept it in check because Sara needed him.

"I didn't even get to go to Maria's funeral," she whispered.

"She knew you loved her." He held her wrists so she couldn't rub the scars anymore. "You did your best, Sara."

"Did I?" She stared at him, her face filled with ragged emotion. "I never tried to leave again. I couldn't stand the thought of another child being hurt because I wasn't there to protect them."

"I read about you on the internet." Compassion for her and the need to be honest in the face of what she'd just revealed forced his confession. "I read how you kept the other kids safe, how you fed them, made sure they did their schoolwork, washed their clothes. You were the best mother they could ever have had."

God had allowed this—atrocity? Kyle's brain simply could not accept that, but this was not the time to say that to her.

"I tried to care for all of them." She dragged her hair off her face as she drew away. "I loved them as much as I could."

"I know." Kyle knew beyond doubt that big-hearted Sara would have showered each child with all the pent-up affection she possessed. She would have protected them, gone to bat for them, had probably even taken their punishment.

"They left, you know. One by one the other kids all left the Masters'." She blinked her spiky lashes and stared into his eyes. "But no one ever came for me."

"Oh, Sara." Kyle had never felt more helpless.

"That's why I needed to find my parents, to ask why they never came back. Now I'll never know." She found a tissue, wiped her eyes and blew her nose. "Maybe someday God will help me find out."

"Sara, how can you still believe in God? How can you trust Him when He didn't get you out of there?" Kyle couldn't have stopped the question if he'd wanted to. Something inside him ached to know what made her so secure in her faith. Some intangible longing made him wonder if he could ever feel that secure in God again.

"God put me there, Kyle." Her wide eyes held his, full of certainty.

"Huh?"

"God put me at the Masters'." She smiled, her heart in her eyes. "If Maria hadn't stopped me from leaving, who would have protected the other kids? Who would have made sure they had a birthday surprise and a Christmas treat? Who would have held them when they were sick and loved them when their parents couldn't?"

"Someone, anyone else?" he snarled, angered by her words.

"No." She reached out and linked her fingers with his. "God gave me a precious opportunity to love those kids." Her laugh at his appalled look echoed around the bay.

"How can you say that?"

"It's not what I'd have chosen," she admitted. "It was miserable and painful and I didn't see it at the time, but I now realize that's why God didn't send my parents to get me. My foster sisters and brothers needed me."

A thousand emotions raced through Kyle: anger, admiration, fury, but most of all a rush of affection. Who wouldn't love this woman?

"Anyway, my past doesn't matter." She slid her hand from his and began to unpack the picnic basket. "I was trying to tell you about…my brother."

"Okay." He waited.

"I thought the dreams were about Maria, but I've finally realized it's not her face I see, it's the face of a little boy with eyes like mine. He holds up his arms, asks me to pick him up. His name is Samuel." Sara's face grew pensive. "I think he's my brother and I intend to find him."

Kyle sat in stunned silence as she called the boys and handed out plates of food. He ate his own sandwich in a bemused fog, trying to absorb what he'd learned, yet not quite ready to deal with the emotions that surged inside.

"Weren't we supposed to go fishing this afternoon, Kyle?"

He blinked back to awareness and saw Barry and Tony standing in front of him. Barry held several rods and reels out from his body as if they were lethal weapons.

"Where did you get those?"

"Lucy and Hector." Tony grinned. "I think they must have some secret source because they keep coming up with stuff for us."

"Their source is God," Sara said calmly. "They pray and God supplies."

"After lunch, we'll see about fishing," Kyle promised.

By the time everyone had finished lunch, he'd been sitting too long with his injured leg in the wrong position. While Sara and the boys cleaned up, Kyle rose, attempting to straighten his knee. A rush of agony surged through him. He overbalanced and would have fallen. But Sara was there, her shoulder strong enough to brace him as he sat again.

"I want you boys to take our lunch things up to Kyle's house and put them in the greenhouse," she said. "I don't want any polar bears getting a whiff of food and stopping by for a visit."

"Kyle said there aren't any here now," one of the boys said. "They've gone till fall."

"The sooner you've finished putting the basket away, the sooner you can fish," she said. "And when you've caught enough fish for dinner tonight, I might be persuaded to give you each a slice of peach pie I made this morning."

"I'm amazed the legal system hasn't thought of using peach pie as a motivator," Kyle muttered, trying to suppress his laughter as the boys hurried away.

"Whatever works." Sara winked at him and extended her hand. Once she'd helped him stand, Kyle eased away from her.

"Thank you for covering for me. It would have been very embarrassing if the kids had seen me land on my kisser."

"You're not going to do that," she assured him. She threaded her arm through his elbow. "While the boys are busy, let's try walking across these rocks. We don't have to hurry."

"I don't think I can—"

"This way." She tugged on his arm just enough to let him know she wasn't giving up.

By the time the boys returned, Kyle was in his favorite fishing spot on the beach and though he'd stumbled and miscalculated his way several times, the boys were none the wiser thanks to Sara's unobtrusive help. Though Kyle's leg ached at the strain of this new activity, his dignity was intact.

Kyle taught the boys to cast, to reel in and to remove the fish they caught. He couldn't remember when he'd enjoyed fishing more. The boys were apt pupils, full of questions and eager to listen to his stories.

It seemed natural for him to return to Lives with them, show them how to clean the fish, and share their dinner.

"That was delicious, Sara." He pushed his plate away, replete.

She pretended to bow. "I never cooked wild meat until someone donated it here, but it made me wonder if sometime you'd show the boys how to hunt? Lucy says Hector has bows and arrows they could use."

"Archery takes a long time to learn," Kyle said. "It's a difficult skill to master."

"Well, they have the time to learn it," she shot back. She disappeared and returned a moment later, bearing the promised pies.

Kyle was amused by the silence that fell while those pies were devoured.

"A guy at school was telling us about sled dog races they have here in the winter," Barry said when everyone had finished seconds. "Do you know about those, Kyle?"

"How about we gather around a campfire to listen to Kyle's story *after* we do cleanup?" Laurel suggested.

Amidst some good-natured grumbling, the boys made the kitchen shipshape while Kyle and Sara built a fire outside.

"Barry's crazy about animals," Sara told him as she chewed on the stem of a straw. Her forehead pleated in a frown. "He wants to be a vet but he's afraid he'd fail the training. I'm searching for a way for him to work with animals so he could build his confidence."

"Your concern to get each of the boys involved in something unique to them makes me think you run this place as much as Laurel does," Kyle teased, delighted when her cheeks turned a bright pink. "I'm not kidding, Sara. You have great insight into what makes these boys tick, more than a lot of professionals would have."

"You just get them to open their hearts," she said. "Then you can see what they really need."

"That's probably easy for you," Kyle mused. "You seem like a natural mother." Maybe not the best thing to say, knowing how much she longed for a family of her own, he thought. "I know a fellow who raises sled dogs. I could ask him if Barry could help out."

"Would you?" Her eyes shone as if she'd been given a prize.

"Sure," he promised.

"I have another favor to ask." Sara glanced over one shoulder as if afraid someone would overhear. "Rod's thirteenth birthday is the day after tomorrow. He really wants to be like his uncle, who I gather was a live-off-the-land man who knew all about nature and survival."

"My kind of guy."

"But far from my realm of experience." She had that gleam in her eye. "I wondered if you'd be willing to arrange some games for the boys that afternoon."

"Games? Such as?" While Kyle admired Sara's determination to help these kids, he recognized that he was getting more involved by the minute.

"I don't know much about games," she said, a

frown appearing. "Maybe you could take them on a hike. Anything to make the day special for him.

"Not a hike, but I'll think of something. You take care of the birthday cake."

"Deal." She held out her hand to shake on it. From her cheeky grin an observer would have thought he'd given her the moon.

"What about you?" he asked. "Are you close to getting your Zodiac ride to see the belugas? They'll be gone in a few weeks, you know."

"Haven't had time yet," she demurred and turned away.

Rod had obviously overheard because he pulled Kyle aside later.

"I don't think Sara will ever go for that ride," the boy confided.

"Why not?" Kyle frowned.

"She keeps using the money she's saving on other people." Rod sighed. "Sara ordered some shoes for an old woman she met at church who can't afford the special ones she needs."

"I see." Kyle waited, knowing there was more Rod wanted to say.

"The guys and I figured we'd pool our allowances and treat her, but we aren't going to have enough to pay for her trip before the whales go. Anyway, the tour operator always says he's booked up."

Sara returned and the conversation ended.

But as the evening progressed, Kyle kept glancing

across the fire at Sara, thinking about what Rod had told him. He pushed those thoughts away as he told the boys stories. Her face beamed as she listened to him talk about the sled dog races held in Churchill every winter.

Sara the giver, the dreamer of possibilities. He'd seen the yearning in her eyes whenever he spoke about the belugas and knew she desperately wanted to fulfill at least that one dream. But even for something so important to her, she was willing to do without so others could have.

What a woman.

As he drove home later, Kyle reflected on the pleasure he'd enjoyed today. He'd never imagined he could get around the beach so easily, let alone reel in a massive sea-run trout as he had in the old days. But he'd landed Tony's twenty-two pounder with no difficulty—once he figured out how to balance himself to counteract the fish's weight.

In fact, the entire day had been a learning experience about his abilities outdoors. The more he tried, the more he'd wanted to try. Except the water. He dreaded the water. The boys had coaxed him to join them for a swim, but Kyle had no desire to plunge into water only to realize he could no longer swim. He'd even had a few anxious moments while the boys were splashing around, worrying that if they got into trouble, he wouldn't be able to help.

Okay, water sports were out. But the rest of it? Thanks to Sara, he was doing just fine.

Kyle stood in his yard, looking out over the bay, and smiled. It wasn't just the birthday party he'd promised to help with. Sara had also coaxed him into teaching the boys wilderness survival techniques, starting tomorrow.

Sara Kane gave a lot. Wasn't it about time somebody made sure her dream came true?

The very thought of climbing into a Zodiac and taking it on the river filled Kyle with trepidation. But today, thanks to Sara, he'd grasped there were some things he could still do. He wouldn't tell her until he was absolutely sure, but as soon as he could get Teddy to help, Kyle intended to start training. If he worked hard enough, he might be able to show Sara the belugas before they left.

He went inside and arranged a time and place with Teddy. But as daylight finally waned, Kyle still wasn't ready to sleep. His brain kept mulling over what Sara had said about God putting her in that foster home.

Kyle switched on his computer. He intended to email whatever contacts he could find to learn why Sara had been removed from her home so many years ago. And while he was at it, he'd start a search for this brother, Samuel. Maybe Sara's longing for a family didn't have to end.

Funny how he'd begun to wish he, too, had someone to share his life with.

At 2:00 a.m., just before he shut down his computer for the night, he shot off one last email to Pastor Rick to ask for another appointment.

Kyle had a lot of questions about God. Maybe it was time to get some answers. He owed Sara that much.

Chapter Eleven

"You did a good job with the tomatoes, Rod." Sara smiled as the boy's shoulders lifted with pride. "It's kind of sad to pull up such productive plants. Next year—" She let the words die away, suddenly aware that she wouldn't be here next year.

And neither would the greenhouse.

Yesterday she'd learned Kyle had received an offer on his house. A pang of sadness at his departure left her feeling down.

"Might as well pull them up. September days are too short for growing," Rod muttered.

Sara could tell by his stare into space that his focus wasn't on removing the tomato vines. "Is anything wrong?" she asked.

He worked for a while longer then faced her. "Can I ask you something?"

"Of course." She smiled to encourage him.

"How do I get a girl to notice me?" Rod asked. A faint pink tinged his cheeks.

"Um, I think that's something you should talk over with Laurel," Sara hedged, feeling totally inept. What did she know of relationships? She'd never even had a crush on a boy before she'd started this crush on Kyle. But Kyle was more than a crush.

"I did ask Laurel." He made a face. "She told me I'm too young. As if I'm thinking about running away to get married. It's just that there's this girl and I like her. But I doubt she even knows I'm alive."

"Have you talked to her?" Sara asked, sending a desperate plea heavenward for help.

"I said hi a couple of times." His face turned redder.

"Maybe next time you see her you should say something more." Desperately aware she didn't have the answers he needed, Sara vowed to search the internet tonight.

This time she would not ask Kyle for help. That was too embarrassing.

"Say something like what?" He scowled. "'I like you?' That sounds dorky."

"Yeah, it does. Maybe you could say you think she's pretty. Or compliment her on what she's wearing." Sara saw the front door of the house open and sighed with relief. *She* didn't have to ask Kyle, but Rod could. "Maybe Kyle could help you with this. Why don't you ask him? A lady at church told me he used to be very popular in school. And he was engaged once."

"Yeah, but Tony told me his fiancée dumped him when he got hurt. That would stink." Rod's forehead wrinkled in thought. "But at least Kyle would know what I should do if this girl gives me the brush-off. Thanks, Sara."

"Good. Maybe don't mention his broken engagement. It might still bother him." She continued pulling tomato vines as Rod pushed open the greenhouse door and welcomed Kyle inside. She didn't want Kyle to know she'd been talking about him.

That was getting to be a habit.

"Harvest is over, huh?" He fingered one of the tomatoes Sara had placed in a basket to take back to Lives.

"'To everything there is a season,'" she quoted, unable to suppress a smile when he rolled his eyes. "Well, it's true."

"Yes, it is. And this season is your birthday. Happy birthday." Kyle's blue eyes met hers and held.

"Thank you," she stammered. "But how did you know?" she asked.

"I'm not telling. But there will be no more work for you today. Right, Rod?" He high-fived the boy.

"Right." Grinning, Rod took the vines from her hands and then hugged her. "Happy birthday, Sara."

"Thank you." She returned his hug, amazed that he allowed it. "But it's just another Saturday. There are chores to do—"

"Nope." Kyle caught her hand and drew her from

the greenhouse, closed the door firmly and stood in front of it. "Today's special."

As if on cue, the other five boys, Laurel, Lucy and Hector came around the corner of the house, singing at the top of their lungs. Their grins grew when a couple of passersby stopped and chimed in.

"Thank you all," Sara said when they were finished. Though embarrassed to be the focus of attention, she treasured their kindness. "You shouldn't go to all this fuss."

"We haven't yet begun to fuss," Kyle assured her. "Get in Laurel's van. We're going for a ride."

With everyone's eyes on her, Sara did as she was told, insisting on sitting in the backseat so Kyle would be more comfortable in the front. The boys were in high spirits, laughing at her and teasing about the sudden approach of old age, distracting her so well that she was surprised when they arrived at the Churchill River.

"The belugas are still here," she whispered as she got out of the van, mesmerized as always by the silent gray shapes gliding through the water.

"Not for long. Another week, maybe." Kyle grinned when Teddy Stonechild climbed out of his truck and gave him a thumbs-up. "So this is your birthday gift, Sara. We're going for a ride on the water so you can see belugas, moms and babies, up close."

"Really?" She stared at him. "But the man who does the tours said—"

"Forget him. Kyle's giving us our own tour. Happy birthday, Sara." Teddy hugged her then motioned to the boys. "Come on, guys."

In short order Kyle launched two inflated boats in the water and started their motors. *Loness's Tours* was printed on the sides of the boats in black lettering. So these were what Kyle and his father had used in their business.

"We'll split into two groups," Kyle directed. "Sara, you'll be with me in that one. Teddy and Laurel will go in the other. We'll split the boys between us." He directed the others into the boats, chuckling when Lucy adamantly refused to go.

"I like my feet on solid ground," she insisted. "I'll watch from here." She plopped onto the tailgate of Teddy's truck.

"Hector?" Kyle grinned at the other man's eager nod and held the boat steady while he boarded.

"Kyle, it's very kind of you," Sara murmured, pausing beside him before she got into the Zodiac. "But are you sure? I know you don't like the water—"

"I didn't," he agreed. His gaze held hers. "But since a certain woman said she wanted to see the whales up close and personal, I've been practicing in the water for a couple of weeks. But if you're worried, you can go with Teddy."

"I'm not worried, Kyle." She grasped his hand and climbed into the dinghy. "I trust you."

Time stopped while his blue eyes searched hers. Sara stared back, willing him to see into her heart, to see the feelings for him that, despite her determination to weed them out, kept growing.

"Having second thoughts, Sara?" Tony called.

"As if!" Sara broke eye contact with Kyle as she took her seat.

After ensuring life jackets were fastened, Kyle climbed in with an ease that surprised her. He sped up the motor, drove to the middle of the river and positioned the boat where he wanted. Teddy followed. Then they cut the motors so that the hush of the afternoon took over.

Sara gasped as the whales swam toward them, curious to see who was in their territory. Beside them, smaller whales crowded their mothers in their eagerness to get close.

"They come here to feed, give birth and molt their skin. They'll be leaving to go south now that the babies are able to take the journey. The males, the bulls, are over there." Kyle pointed. "We won't go near because they're hunting. They swim round and round like that to draw the fish into their circle. Watch."

Sara gasped when all at once the males plunged into the middle of the circle, somehow avoiding each other as they dove after the fish they'd corralled. She felt the boat move as Kyle sat beside her.

"Let your hand trail in the water," he suggested. His breath felt warm against her ear.

The belugas looked huge next to their puny boat. After witnessing the hunt, Sara feared the mothers and babies would go into the same feeding frenzy and cause their craft to upset. She gazed into Kyle's eyes and knew beyond a shadow of a doubt that he wouldn't let anything happen to her. She dipped her fingers into the chilly water. Almost instantly a cool wet nose pushed against her hand.

"Oh, my." She gasped, freezing for a moment before she slid her hand along the baby whale's back as it swam past. Her heart in her mouth, she skimmed her fingertips over its tail fin. The boys mirrored her actions and soon they were surrounded by whales eager to have their heads, their snouts and their blowholes touched.

"It's amazing. To think God created such wonder as this."

Sara turned her head to thank Kyle and found his lips inches from hers. Suddenly she couldn't say anything, could only feel the press of his strong shoulder against her back and the gentleness of his hand where it rested against her waist.

Is this love? I never dreamed I could feel so light, so happy.

Was this odd tingling, this desire to lean an inch closer and press her lips to his—was that love?

Sara didn't know. She only knew that Kyle's gift of this incredible afternoon meant he'd taken time to relearn what he'd feared he'd never do again. And he'd done it for her. Did that mean he cared about her, even the tiniest bit?

"Thank you, Kyle," she whispered. "This is the best birthday gift anyone could have given me."

"I'm glad. But the day is just beginning." He grinned before moving back to his seat by the motor. With infinite patience he waited until each boy had his fill of touching the incredible beings.

More than once Sara caught herself staring at Kyle, admiring the proud way he held himself, the agility he'd regained.

"Now we could go over to the Prince of Wales Fort and take a look around, if you want."

Kyle grinned when she and the boys whooped their answer.

He gunned the motor, speeding them across the river. Sara turned her head into the wind, loving the brisk, refreshing air that tugged her hair back, and allowed the heat of the autumn sun to warm her.

"Couldn't have picked a better day for a birthday," Teddy called as they moored the Zodiacs. "Good work, Sara."

She laughed at Teddy, but her breath caught in her throat as Kyle teetered on the edge of the dock, almost losing his balance as he dragged the Zodiac to a drier landing area. He caught her stare and grinned.

"Don't worry. I practiced this part a lot," he joked. He held out a hand to help her disembark. The others surged toward the fort, leaving them to trail behind. "Come on. It's an old place but it's interesting."

Sara listened with rapt attention as Kyle showed her the weathered remains of a rough stone dwelling house, the men's barracks, the storehouse, the stonemason's and carpenter's workshops, a tailor's room and a blacksmith's shop.

"Each of them had a huge part in making this settlement viable," he said. "I've always admired their courage in staying."

"And in bringing their families here," she mused. She touched his arm. "I can't thank you enough for this gift, Kyle."

"You already have." He tucked her arm in his. "Come on. I want to show you the view across the river to Cape Merry."

Sara went eagerly, not even trying to suppress the thrill that walking next to him, hearing the rumble of his voice, watching him move with confidence and assurance, brought.

She sent a silent prayer of thanksgiving that Kyle was finally healing.

Kyle stood on his back step and soaked in the pleasure of having a crowd of happy people in his backyard. It had been too long since he'd laughed so hard.

"Was today worth all your training?" Teddy asked between bites of his hot dog.

"Do you expect me to say you were right to keep pushing me?" Kyle grinned. "You were right," he admitted.

"Of course I was," Teddy said smugly. "Sara seems to be enjoying the day."

"I hope so. She deserves it." Kyle ignored the hint in Teddy's tone.

"Yeah, she does. She's a nice lady. You could do worse," Teddy hinted.

"I did, remember?" Kyle shot him a glare. "I'm not getting involved with Sara. Marriage isn't for me. I think I've proven that. And it's doubly out of the question now. You know why."

"Because you made a bad choice and got dumped?"

"That's not the only reason, though it's a good one."

"Because you can't have kids?" Teddy shook his head. "Doctors don't know everything, Kyle. Didn't you see what happened today? Sara couldn't stop staring at you. She came alive because of you, because of what you did."

"I haven't got anything to offer, Teddy. I don't have a job. I won't have a home. I haven't even got Dad's affairs settled yet." When Sara sent him a quizzical look from the breakfast trays, Kyle smiled back automatically. "Besides, she's leaving after Christmas."

"I certainly hope you've got enough guts not to let her leave." Teddy strode away.

"Something wrong?" Sara handed him a cup of coffee. "He seems upset."

"Teddy likes to give advice. He doesn't like it when I refuse to take it."

"Listen, Kyle. I've been wanting to tell you something all day." She paused, licked her lips and allowed a faint smile to crease her lips. "I might have found my brother. Samuel."

Kyle could hear her hesitation and knew she was afraid her hopes would be dashed again. He hated seeing fear dim her gorgeous eyes. He wanted to chase the shadows away, watch her laugh again.

"Are you sure it's him?"

"Not yet." She grinned. "I checked Facebook for his name and found him. I asked Rod to friend him—is that how you say it?"

"Yes. And?" Kyle wanted to hear all of it.

"His birthdate, his coloring and especially his eyes all make me think he's my brother." Her face glowed. "He looks a bit like me, Rod says."

"Oh." A sudden urge to protect Sara overtook Kyle. What if this guy was some kind of creep? He didn't say that, however, because he knew Sara would tell him to trust God.

"He doesn't say anything about being adopted and he uses the same last name as me, so I do think it's him." She could hardly contain her excitement. "Isn't it wonderful?"

"It is," he agreed. "So what will you do?"

"I'm not sure." Sara's gorgeous eyes dipped to avoid his.

"Today is your day. Anything is possible." Kyle tipped up her chin and stared into her eyes.

"Do you really think so?" she whispered.

"Yes." How desperately he wanted her to finally achieve this dream. Kyle had to ensure she didn't let fear dissuade her. "You've come this far," he said in a very gentle tone. "Don't give up now. Trust God. Isn't that what you're always telling me?"

"Yes." Her smile was tentative.

Kyle brushed his fingers against her cheek. "You've been a warrior since you came here. That's what we all love about you."

"Really? I don't know."

Kyle nodded.

"If I need help," she began.

"I'll be there. All you have to do is call," Kyle assured her.

"Thank you." Her voice came whisper soft.

For a moment, it seemed as if they were in a world of their own. Communication, unspoken but nevertheless full of meaning, flowed between them.

Kyle understood that disappointment from her

past searches for her family had left her feeling insecure, afraid to try again.

He also understood that she could not turn away from this chance to meet the last member of her family if it was at all possible.

Most of all, Kyle understood that he wanted Sara to have everything her heart desired.

"You're a strong, fiercely courageous woman who has God on her side," he whispered as Rod walked toward them. "Don't change it now."

She held his gaze. Nothing changed and yet, in the fraction of a second, everything did. Hesitation, fear—whatever it was—drained away. She stood straight and tall, her head held high.

"I'm going to do it," she told him. She reached out and squeezed his hand. "Thank you."

"Anytime."

"Excuse me, Sara. I need to talk to Kyle. Privately." Rod waited as Sara let go of his hand. She nodded once then walked away.

Kyle hated to have that moment end. He turned to Rod, stuffed down his frustration and asked, "What do you need?"

"The cake? You said I should find you about this time. Remember?"

Kyle nodded. Turning, he moved as fast as he could up the ramp and inside his house.

Rod met him at the top. "So what should I do?"

"Follow me." Kyle led him into the kitchen. "Open the fridge."

Rod did and whistled as he lifted out a massive cake. "Wow!"

"Sara said she'd never had a birthday cake. Imagine." Kyle shook his head. "A woman like Sara should have a cake to celebrate her birthday. So I ordered a big chocolate one."

"There's enough for seconds. Maybe even thirds," Rod enthused. He inserted the candles and Kyle lit them.

"Okay, I'll go first. Then you come behind me with the cake and please, don't drop it," he told the boy.

"If it's chocolate, no worries, mate. I don't waste chocolate." Rod followed him, waiting inside the house until Kyle called for attention. Right on cue, Rod stepped through the door while Kyle led everyone in singing "Happy Birthday" as Rod carried the massive cake to Sara and set it in front of her with a gallant flourish.

Sara's eyes grew huge as the flames sputtered in a tiny draft off the water. "You did this?" she asked, looking directly at Kyle.

"He didn't make it, so it's edible," Teddy joked.

"You had to have a birthday cake," Kyle said quietly.

"Blow out the candles, Sara," Laurel urged.

"Make a wish first," Tony insisted.

Kyle couldn't break away from Sara's silver-gray stare. It felt as if she spun a web about him, holding him in its grasp until she squeezed her eyes closed. A hush fell on the group as she took a deep breath, opened her eyes and blew out all the candles.

Everyone cheered. As she cut slices of cake for the clamoring group, Kyle suddenly knew that he wanted someone in his life, someone to share everything with, someone to be there for the tough spots and the happy ones.

Not just someone. Sara. He wanted Sara, with her shining face, beautiful smile and gentle heart.

And just as surely as that sweet knowledge came to him, he knew he could never have that relationship with Sara, even if he dared ask her.

How could he subject this caring, giving woman to a lifetime of being shortchanged because he couldn't do anything she wanted or needed? He'd had to practice like crazy just to be able to get those Zodiacs on the water. He needed help all the time. How could he ever be the kind of husband a wonderful woman like Sara deserved?

It was more than being disabled and Kyle knew it. Below all the doubts about his ability to ever be "normal" again lay a fact that no amount of physical therapy, exercise or prayer could change. It was what kept him from losing himself in his dreams of happily-ever-after. It was what restrained him from becoming dependent on Sara's quick-flash smile to cheer him, or the steady encouragement she offered. It kept him from getting snagged in the "can do it" attitude Sara Kane bequeathed on everyone.

Sweet, loving Sara wanted a family. And according to what the doctors had told him about the bomb blast he'd survived, the shrapnel had pretty well made sure Kyle couldn't give her one. Not ever. That was why he couldn't reconcile God and love. That was why he still fought to understand why. That was why he had to leave this place and start over somewhere else.

"Kyle?" Sara stood before him, arm outstretched, holding a big slice of her cake. "Are you okay?" she asked, head tilted sideways.

"Yes." He took the cake. "Thanks."

"This has been a wonderful day."

"Good," he said, irritated by the longing to pull her into his arms. "Just enjoy it."

"I am." She frowned. "Was it very difficult to relearn the skills you needed with the boats?"

"Yes," he said. "And no. It wasn't that hard after I made up my mind I was going to do it. Getting to that stage was a little more difficult."

"I told—"

"Do not even think about saying 'I told you so,'" he warned.

"Okay." She chuckled and his glower evaporated. "Can I ask you something else instead?"

"You can ask," he said slowly.

"If I wrote to my brother, do you think he'd be mad or would he want to talk to me?" She waited eagerly for his answer.

"Sara, I can't tell you that. I don't know him. I don't know how he'd react." The light went out of her face.

"I know. I just thought maybe—" She shrugged and stopped.

Kyle wasn't going to let it go at that. She deserved more from him.

"I'll tell you this. You'll never know unless you write him and ask," he said, watching the way she ducked her head to hide her gaze from him. "I'm guessing you have an address for him?"

"Yes. But what if he doesn't want to talk to me? What if he has another family now?" She was full into her what-ifs. It hurt Kyle to listen to the anxiety in her voice.

"What if he's thrilled to hear from you and wants to see you as soon as possible?" he countered. "What if he's been looking for you ever since you were kids?"

"You think?" Eagerness lit up her lovely face.

"You never know."

As the day cooled and the sun lowered, the party came to a close. Sara was the last to say good-night. Kyle froze when she threw her arms around his neck and hugged him.

"I don't know how I can ever thank you for such a wonderful birthday," she murmured into his ear.

The sweet softness of her embrace, the quiet whisper of her voice, the feeling that he'd finally come home—all of these overwhelmed Kyle in a rush. Slowly, almost of their own accord, his arms lifted to encircle her waist. Her cheek brushed his, like a whisper of velvet, and all he could do was stand there.

Her lips grazed the corner of his mouth where his scar cut through, then she drew away. "Thank you, Kyle."

"My pleasure" was all he could manage as he watched her slip away.

Long after everyone had gone, Kyle stood in his backyard alone, remembering that moment and wishing, praying, it could happen again.

Why tempt me with something I can't have? Why am I here? What do You want from me?

When no answer came, he went inside, picked up his phone and dialed Pastor Rick. Maybe talking would help, maybe it wouldn't. But a desperate need to understand God ate at him.

"I'm making the first move," he muttered as he stared at a tiny ribbon of green light that was winding its way across the eastern sky. "The rest is up to You."

Chapter Twelve

Sara stood transfixed as the bugler played "The Last Post" during the November 11 Remembrance Day ceremony. The touching observance honoring those who'd fought and died to save Canada drew her tears. This date had never struck her as deeply as it did today, especially with Kyle at her side.

During the Veterans Day lunch that followed, Kyle, seemed unusually silent, as if sobered by memories of friends he'd lost. Later, Sara drove him to his house in Laurel's van, unsure of how to break the silence.

"Who taught you to drive?" he asked when she'd parked in front of his place.

"Laurel. I didn't want to learn, but she insisted. And I'm glad she did. I'll need that skill when I leave."

He glanced at her as if to say something then quickly looked away.

"The for-sale sign is still up," she said in surprise.

"The first offer fell through." Kyle didn't sound especially bothered about that, for which Sara was glad. It meant he wasn't eager to leave, didn't it?

"Thanks for coming with me today." He reached out for the door handle then paused. "Are you busy this afternoon?"

"No." His hesitant demeanor surprised Sara—Kyle was never hesitant. "What do you need?"

"A…friend." He glanced at her over his shoulder. "A good friend. I want to scatter my dad's ashes today."

"Kyle, I'm honored you'd ask me to do that with you." She laid a hand on his arm, meaning every word. A little thrill ran through her that he felt close enough to her to share this farewell to his beloved father. "Do you want to go right away?"

"Yes." He studied her. "But you'll need warmer clothes. The jacket is okay but—"

"I have my snow pants in the van," she said. "I should order a new coat and return this one of your mother's—"

"I gave it to you. Keep it," he said. "Come on. You can put on your snow pants while I get my ski suit on."

"Okay." She trudged through the snow behind him. Once inside she blinked in surprise at the emptiness of the kitchen. "It feels so big in here."

"I guess you haven't been in here in a while. I've

taken out a lot of stuff." He grinned. "When you first came here and moved stuff around, it made me realize how much room there could be."

"You've done a great job," she said, sliding her fingers across a highboy. "I didn't notice this before. It's lovely."

"Yeah. Mom insisted we bring it back with us after our term in Pakistan. It cost a fortune but Dad had given it to her for Christmas one year and she wouldn't leave it behind."

"Did you like living there?" she asked, studying the intricate work.

"Yes. I had a lot of friends and there was always something interesting to do." He found his outdoor gear.

"It must have been hard to move here," she murmured, thinking of the little boy who'd left behind everything familiar.

"With Dad in the military, I was used to moving. Plus my parents always made relocating sound like a big adventure." He paused, his gaze faraway. "Churchill feels like home." Kyle roused himself after a minute and shrugged. "I'll go change out of my uniform."

"I'm glad you wore it to the ceremony. You look really good in it," she told him, shyly determined to let Kyle hear her admiration. "You represented your part of the forces so well. The whole service was wonderful. I've never seen anything like that before," she murmured.

"You've never been to a Remembrance Day service?" he asked, one eyebrow raised.

"Last year I went by myself but it wasn't like today." Feeling childish, she kept her eyes downcast. "I never understood it. My foster parents never talked about people who served to keep our country safe."

"Why doesn't that surprise me?" Kyle muttered before he disappeared into his room to change clothes.

Sara stared after him for a moment, wondering how much he'd learned about her life in the foster home when he'd looked her up online.

After a moment, she shrugged it off and pulled on her snow pants. This day was about Kyle's dad, not her wretched past. She stared at the lean, angled face of the man in the picture on the wall and wished she'd known Matt Loness.

God, I don't have many weeks left here. Please help me help him, she prayed silently.

When Kyle emerged from the bedroom he wore jeans, thick socks and a flannel shirt.

"Ready?" he asked as he dragged on his snowsuit.

"Yes." She zipped up the red jacket he'd lent her. It still felt like a warm hug, but it was nothing compared to being in Kyle's arms. Pushing away her longing, she pulled up the hood. "Will we walk?"

"No. I want to go up on the cliffs and I'm not sure how much I can handle in all this snow. I thought we could take the snowmobile if you don't mind riding behind and holding this." He lifted a small black box off the table. "I can put it in my knapsack if you'd rather not—"

"I'd be honored." Her smile died when she saw him pull a small handgun out of a metal safe. "What's that for?"

"Bears. Just in case. I have a whistle, as well." He tucked both in his pocket. "Shall we go?"

She followed him outside. A snowmobile sat at the side of his house. It started with one pull.

"Tony got this old thing running. He's got a great future as a mechanic if he wants it," Kyle said over the roar of the motor. He helped her straddle the seat. While Sara clasped the box with both hands, Kyle slid a helmet on her head, fastened it then put on his own. She made herself small, trying to leave enough room for him to sit in front of her, but she was soon glad of his broad back as, a moment later, they went gliding over the snow toward the cliffs.

Filled with trepidation at first, Sara gradually relaxed and found she loved the ride, even when she had to grab hold of Kyle with one hand to keep from falling off. The world seemed like a downy white quilt spread around them. She wondered how far they'd go.

Once on the cliffs, Kyle slowed down as if he

was trying to find exactly the right spot. Finally he stopped the snowmobile on a huge, wind-hardened drift that overlooked the bay. He climbed off then held out a hand.

"Dad loved to come and sit here in the summer. He called it his thinking spot. I think this will do." Once she'd stepped off, he removed his helmet and set it on the seat. Then he took the box from her. "I'm going to walk closer to the edge but you don't have to come."

"Of course I'm coming." Sara removed her own helmet before following, matching her steps with his. When he faltered on a rough patch, she slid her arm through his and pretended she needed his guidance.

"This is the place," Kyle said when they'd gone about a hundred yards.

Sara caught her breath at the vista. Below her the land dropped away to water, which shone like polished glass. Tufts of snow jutted up in icy peaks covered by froth.

"I'm guessing we'll have an early freeze-up this year," Kyle said.

"Is that good?"

"I guess it depends on your viewpoint," he said. "The tourists like to see the polar bears but when the ice locks in, the bears leave. Don't let that ice fool you, though. It's not thick yet. At these temperatures it will take about another week before it's safe to walk on."

Sara glanced around. She'd seen polar bears many times since she'd first arrived. Though she marveled at their beauty, she was in awe of the strength and the power of their massive jaws.

"Relax. I haven't seen any signs," he said with a half smile. "You're safe."

"Polar bears make me think of that verse, 'Fearfully and wonderfully made,'" she told him.

But Kyle's attention was on the small box. He took off his gloves and tucked them under his arm before lifting the lid.

The afternoon seemed to suddenly still. A hush fell. Sara could hear the crackle of the ice and little else. The skies were turning that leaden gray tone that she'd learned meant snow was imminent. Everything seemed to wait.

"Well, Dad," Kyle finally said very softly, "I brought you back to the place you loved the most. I know you're happier now that you're in heaven with Mom, but—I miss you." The last three words burst out of him as if he could no longer contain them. He blinked his eyes hard then murmured, "Goodbye, Dad. I love you."

Sara held her breath as he lifted his arm and slowly tipped the box. A zephyr wind skipped across the snow from behind them. It caught the ashes and carried them in a trail out over the water, where they disappeared and became part of the landscape. She tipped her head up as huge fat snowflakes began to tumble from the heavens.

When she looked at Kyle, he looked bereft, utterly sad and totally alone.

"Your father would have loved hearing what you said," she told him.

"How do you know?" His voice cracked as he dashed away a tear.

"What father wouldn't love a tribute like that from his beloved son?" When he'd pulled on his gloves, Sara again slipped her arm through his, wanting to show him that she was there for him, to ease his pain if he'd let her.

"I miss him." Those three words emerged in a cracked and strained voice. He pulled her tightly against him and buried his face in her neck. "I miss him so much."

"I know." Sara held him, feeling the sobs heave his chest and knowing this release had been a long time coming. She smoothed his hair with her gloved fingers and waited. When he finally quieted, she eased his head up so she could see his face. "But your father is still with you. You carry him inside your heart, Kyle."

He looked at her for a very long time.

"Only you would say that." He leaned forward

and pressed his icy lips against hers, asking, giving, loving.

Stunned at first, Sara did her best to respond, to show him how special he was to her. She knew nothing of the proper way to kiss a man. But she knew that she loved kissing this one. She only knew it felt right to melt into Kyle's arms, to express all that he had come to mean to her. So she kissed him back as her heart overflowed with love.

"How do you do it, Sara?" Kyle asked as he at last drew away, his arms still circled around her. "How do you always know exactly the right thing to say to make me feel better?"

"Do you feel better?" she asked timidly.

"Yes, I do." He brushed his lips against her forehead and let them rest there, lost in his thoughts. Some moments later he said, "Dad was spared pain and suffering. He died in a place he loved among those he loved. And they loved him." He lifted his head. His thumbs pressed her tousled hair off her face. "It would be selfish to wish he'd stayed. And you're right, he is in my heart. Even after I leave here, that won't change." His arms dropped away and it was like a frigid arctic air mass had moved in.

"Do you have to leave?" Sara peered up at him, wishing, praying he'd say no.

"I can't stay in Churchill." He turned and led the way to the snowmobile. "What would I do?"

"What you have been doing," she said. "Work at Lives helping the kids, being a part of the community."

"And live on what?" He handed her a helmet. "Laurel can't afford to pay me even if I was qualified to work with the boys. Which I'm not."

"She's working on a grant to add positions at Lives," Sara told him. "Maybe—"

"I can't live here anymore, Sara."

She swallowed hard but she could not stifle the words. "You belong here," she pleaded, praying he'd agree.

"Maybe once, but not anymore." He drew a ragged breath. "It's too hard to know I'll never be able to take guests snowshoeing, to know that I will never be able to take anyone hunting or teach them to track. It's killing me to see everything I've always loved and know I can't do it anymore."

"Why can't you?" she demanded. "You took us in the Zodiacs."

"It took me ages to figure out how to do that," he said.

"You don't have time?" Sara wasn't giving up no matter how he glared at her.

"I had Teddy to help me that day," Kyle growled. "I can't expect him to come running every time I need help."

New insight dawned in Sara's mind.

"That's what your decision to leave is really about,

isn't it?" She shook her head, amazed she hadn't seen it before. "You feel you'll become dependent if you let someone help you."

"Yes, that's it. Okay?" His angry outburst echoed around them. "I can no longer rely on me. And I hate that."

He glared at her so fiercely, Sara should have been frightened. Instead, her heart wept.

Oh, Kyle, if you only understood how much joy it gives others to help you. Especially me.

"Get on the snowmobile, Sara," he said, his voice resigned. "I want to go home."

"Of course you do," she said, facing him. "Because it *is* home. And home is where you belong, Kyle. It's where we all belong." She forced a smile. "By the way, just so you know, no one can completely rely on themselves. Everyone needs God in their lives."

She knew from his obstinate look that she couldn't change his mind so she climbed on behind him and wrapped her arms around his waist, praying for him as they glided over the snow.

At his house Kyle jerked the machine to a halt and pulled off his knapsack. "Thanks for coming," he growled.

"Wait a minute." She pulled on his arm, forcing him to stop. "We have some things to talk about."

"What things?" Kyle went up the ramp and inside

with Sara behind him. He shucked off his outdoor clothes then flopped into a chair.

"You kissed me," she began haltingly.

"Yeah." He looked at her and her heart began to race at the flash in his blue eyes. "That shouldn't have happened."

Her heart stopped. "Wh-why?"

"It was a reaction thing. I was—upset and you comforted me and—" He shrugged.

"I was in the right place at the right time. Is that what you're saying?" She glared at him.

"Sara, I cannot have a relationship with you."

Why wasn't she smarter? Why didn't she know the right words to say?

"Why can't you have a relationship with me?"

"I'm a crippled guy who hasn't figured out how to handle life on his own, let alone with someone else. I'm trying but I have a long way to go before I'll be able to fully trust God again." He rose and began pacing, a flicker of anguish tightening his mouth.

"Look at me. I can't even carry two cups to the table without worrying if I'll spill one."

"And you think that matters?" She got up, carried her own cup to the table and sat down again. "Independence is a great thing, Kyle, until you shut everyone out. Please don't shut me out. I care about you. I—I love you."

There, she'd bared her heart. Saying the words had terrified her. She'd never opened up to anyone as she had to this man. But though she was scared of his reaction, she was also proud of her feelings, glad that her heart had chosen him.

"Sara." Kyle sat down then shook his head. "You can't."

She was suddenly angry. "Why?"

"Because you've never had a relationship, have you?" He nodded when she shook her head. "You don't know what love is."

"Really?" She glared at him. "Wasn't it you who told me, not too long ago, that I knew more about love than most people?" She shook her head at him. "Forget the condescension, Kyle. I may be inexperienced, but I do know what's in my heart. I love you. You're just going to have to deal with it."

Kyle stared at her for a moment, obviously surprised. Sara held his gaze, refusing to back down. Finally he spoke.

"I wasn't trying to hurt you. I was trying to say that you might be mistaken."

"I'm not."

"Sara, you're leaving in a month and a half." A desperate pleading filled his voice. "You've got a chance to live the life you want. You'll find someone special, someone who can love you the way you need."

"Someone like you," she whispered, her heart plummeting at every word.

"No." Kyle shook his head. "Someone the opposite of me." He sighed, rubbed his knee. "If I were going to have a relationship, I'd want it to be with someone like you, Sara. But I can't."

"Because you're afraid you'll get hurt again?" Her boldness amazed her.

"Because I have nothing to give anyone."

Sara sat very still, taking in all that Kyle had just said, trying to understand the truth that lay behind his words and fend off the deep hurt he'd caused. Finally she said, "My brother hasn't answered my letter yet. I guess he's like you. He doesn't want me, either."

"I'm sorry." He moved, as if he'd enfold her in his arms again then stopped himself. "Give him time. I'm sure he'll change his mind."

"Like you will?" she asked. He didn't answer. "I don't think God is going to give me my family, Kyle. I don't think it's His will. The thing is, I can't figure out what His will for me *is*. I thought I'd find it here. That's why I came. I was so sure—" She dashed away her tears as she stared out the window at the snowmobile covered in fresh snowflakes.

"Sara, please talk to me," Kyle said in a low, intense voice.

She smiled at him even as her heart wondered how she'd manage when he was no longer there to talk to. When she was alone.

"What are you thinking?"

"That I now understand the allure of that machine," she murmured. "That ride today—it must be wonderful to get on and go be alone in the wilderness with your thoughts."

"Would you like to learn to drive it?"

"What?" Sara stared at Kyle. "Are you serious?"

"Why not?" He shrugged. "Might come in handy someday."

"I'd love it."

He rose. "Come on. Let's go have your first lesson. I doubt you'll need more than one."

It felt good to move, to break, to escape the tension her admission of love had brought to the room. But the thought of driving that powerful machine terrified her. Heart in her throat, Sara pulled on her warm clothes and followed Kyle outside. The snowmobile sat there, big and intimidating, but offering a whole new world to explore.

"You start it like this." He made her repeat the process several times then listed the rules and made her repeat them back to him.

The entire time Sara struggled to keep her focus off the way Kyle's hand felt covering hers, the way his smile lit up the blue in his eyes, the way his broad shoulders behind her made her feel safe, protected when he took his seat behind her. He was so gentle, so tender and patient. She had to keep reminding herself that this was the man who had just said he could never love her.

"I think you're ready. Head that way." He pointed toward the cliffs where they'd been earlier.

Sara felt his shoulders shake when she pushed the throttle too hard and the machine jerked forward. Embarrassed, she bit her lip and tried again. After several attempts, she soon had the knack of slowing for bumps and crossing trails. Bit by bit she revved the engine to move faster. Okay, he'd said he couldn't love her. But he couldn't stop her from treasuring these precious moments alone with Kyle in this vast, white wilderness.

He directed her past the grain terminal and out of town. Unsure of their destination, Sara followed his directions. Soon they were in the middle of nowhere with only shrubs and the river distinguishing the landscape. Lost in the beauty, she was startled when Kyle asked her to stop.

"Did I do something wrong?"

"No. You did fine," he assured her. "I need to stand for a few minutes." He winced as he tried to stand.

"Wait." Sara climbed off and held out a hand. He hesitated. She debated a moment then said, "Helping someone else makes the other person feel useful, you know."

Finally he grasped her hand to leverage himself upright.

Sara took off her helmet and tipped her face into the falling snowflakes. "I think this is the loveliest place on earth," she whispered and turned to find Kyle directly in front of her.

"Wait till it hits minus-forty degrees," Kyle said, his lips mere inches from her ear.

Sara wanted so badly to feel his arms wrap around her, to be loved. But Kyle didn't want that. Apparently neither did God. She stepped away from him, needing the space to assemble her troubled thoughts.

Sara had overheard Laurel hiring a new cook on the phone this morning. Now, standing here in the snow, she suddenly realized she'd changed her mind, that she wanted to stay on at Lives, at least for as long as Kyle was here. Maybe if she was here long enough he'd change his mind.

But she'd given her promise that she would leave before the New Year began, insisted Laurel not let her change her mind. How could she now make a fuss and force everyone to change their plans?

"See over there, that cove in the river? That's where my buddies and I used to come to fish." Kyle stood beside her, his head bare. "And over there, where the hill rises, we'd haul deadwood over to make a fort. There aren't many trees in Churchill, most grow along the river. We'd shinny up the largest ones and pretend we were settlers sighting French ships in the bay."

"That sounds like fun," she murmured.

"It was. That rock with the oddly shaped top? That's Top Hat Rock. And that is an abandoned stone house." He grinned. "We had a lot of fun playing hide-and-seek there."

Sara could see it in her mind, a younger Kyle, happy and carefree.

"What are you thinking?" he asked.

"That I envy you."

"Why?" His eyes grew dark and stormy. "Because your past was so miserable? I'm sorry, I shouldn't—"

"Don't." She put her fingers over his lips, relishing this bit of intimacy. "Don't be sorry that you had a wonderful home and family that loved you. Don't ever be sorry that you knew such blessings. Anyway, that isn't what I meant." She withdrew her fingers slowly, knowing that she had no right to touch him like that, no matter what her heart wanted.

"Then what?"

"I meant I envy you because you've done so much, seen so much." She smiled. "You know so many things that I haven't got a clue about."

"You've driven a snowmobile." He flashed his devastating smile. His soft voice soothed. "You live what you believe and you pass it on to everyone around you. You fit perfectly wherever you go, Sara."

"Thank you for saying that, Kyle." She tilted her head to one side and smiled. "So I guess you'd agree that God has blessed both of us?"

Sara watched carefully for some sign of anger. She didn't find it. Instead, after a long pause, Kyle nodded, his gaze on something far ahead, which she couldn't see.

"I guess maybe He has," he murmured. "Come on. It's time to go back before it gets dark. Try to remember as many landmarks as you can in case you get lost someday."

"I doubt that will happen," Sara said as she climbed on the machine and drove them back. As she drove, she offered a prayer of thanksgiving that at last Kyle had begun to reconcile his faith. Had he finally begun to see God as the Giver of Life, maybe even of his future?

But even though she was delighted for him, Sara was suddenly struck by the pain his rejection brought, and struggled not to feel devastated. But the man she loved didn't want her in his future. There was no escaping that.

When will You bring love into my life? When will You show me what You want me to do? When will I get Kyle out of my heart?

The silence of the blanketed land offered no answers.

They hit a soft spot and dipped. Sara gripped the handlebars, bracing herself. The snow came harder now, with gusts of headwinds that buffeted them and made visibility difficult. She paused once when Kyle tapped her shoulder.

"You're doing really well, Sara. I just wanted to mention something."

She nodded.

"You see how it's beginning to storm? When the wind really gets going it will be much harder to see. Storms up here can cause white-out conditions."

"It's almost that now," she said, peering through the whirling snow.

"It can get much worse than this. Lots of people get lost in it. Do you remember rule number one?"

"If you get lost, stop, dig a snow fort and take refuge inside while you wait for someone to find you," she repeated, almost yelling to make herself heard above the wind.

"Exactly." He nodded and pointed to the right, showing that she'd gone off track. "Go that way. We're almost home."

Almost home?

Where is my home, God? Sara asked over and over.

She heard only one word in her heart.

Trust.

Chapter Thirteen

Kyle caught himself whistling a Christmas carol as he drove his sled to Pastor Rick's. Their talks were helping him finally shed the anger that had clung to his shoulders ever since his father had died. But he wasn't there yet. He said that to Rick.

"Let go and keep your mind open," his new friend advised. "God has a plan, even if you don't know what it is yet. In the meantime, the help, encouragement and role modeling you do for the boys at Lives are making a difference. You realize, don't you, that it's because of your dad that you find it so easy to teach them survival skills?"

"How do you figure?"

"Because that's what your father did for you, Kyle. He taught you to figure things out, to find a way to do what you want." Rick's grin was irrepressible. "Isn't that how you figured out how you can snowshoe with your bad leg?"

"Yeah, I guess it is. Dad always used to say that if you wanted something enough, nothing could stop you." Kyle grinned.

"That's his legacy to you," Rick said. "Strength, grit and determination. You were entrusted with that so you could pass it on to these kids. They need to know that their past isn't going to hold them back, that if they want to and are willing to work at it, they can change their lives."

"I think Sara's pretty well drummed that into them, but I'm happy to do what I can to help out."

"How is Sara? I missed her at church on Sunday," Rick said.

"That might be my fault." Even as he said it, a ton of guilt rose in Kyle. "I think she's avoiding me."

"Why?" Rick listened as he explained what had happened the day he'd spread his father's ashes.

"I had to reject her," Kyle told him.

"Why? From what you've told me, I thought you had feelings for her." Rick inclined his head. "What's wrong with that."

"Nothing can come of it."

"Because you don't want to get involved? Because you don't want to take a chance on loving again, in case you're rejected?" The way Rick said it sounded silly.

"Sara wouldn't reject me because of my leg," Kyle told him and knew it was true. "She's not like that."

"So the issue is—you don't want to take any risks

with her, just like you didn't want to take any risks with God. And look how that turned out." Rick shook his head. "You're looking for guarantees, Kyle, and in this life there aren't any. You're going to have to decide what's important to you. If Sara is important then I suggest you figure out a way to make amends." He shook his head. "I don't know a woman in the world who wouldn't be hurting if they got the rejection you described."

They spent a while praying, then Kyle left, troubled by the words he'd said to her, the way he'd spurned her. He still didn't think a relationship between them was possible, but he needed her friendship.

"And I gave Teddy advice about Laurel," he muttered to himself as he drove to Lives. "Practice what you preach, dummy."

The first thing he was going to do was apologize to Sara. But it turned out not to be that easy. He found her in the kitchen, stirring a pot that gave off the most delicious aroma. How to begin?

"What's that?"

"The filling for chicken pie. I'm making one for Christmas morning—" The last word came out on a wail. Sara sank into a kitchen chair, weeping so loudly Kyle thought his heart would break.

With great difficulty he knelt in front of her, pushed her hair back and peered into her eyes, panicked by her tears and the hopelessness he heard in her voice. "Sara? What's wrong?"

Silver eyes brimming with tears, she looked at him and laid a hand over her heart. "It hurts so badly, Kyle. How can I make it stop?"

"What happened?" He waited as she reached into her apron pocket and pulled out a crumpled piece of paper. Without saying a word she held it out.

Kyle unfolded it. Slowly he read the harsh, condemning words her brother had written, damning claims that Sara had abandoned him to suffer growing up with no one to watch out for him as a big sister should. When Kyle came to Samuel's demand to be left alone, to his insistence that he wanted nothing to do with his sister, a gut-wrenching ache tore through him. The last link to Sara's precious family had been severed.

"It's okay, Sara," he murmured, touching her hand.

"It is *not* okay, Kyle." She snatched back the letter and shoved it into her pocket. "Samuel is my brother, my last living link with our family. How can I just let him go?"

The last word emerged on a sob that shook her. Kyle's heart wrenched at her grief when she stared at him through tear-glazed eyes.

"How will it ever be okay?" she mourned.

With great difficulty, Kyle rose. He leaned over and drew her into his arms.

"I don't know, Sara," he murmured. "Only God

knows." She fit perfectly in his arms and suddenly Kyle longed to have the right to be the one to comfort her forever.

Because he loved her.

The knowledge sucker punched Kyle. He didn't say a word; he couldn't have.

He'd cared about Sara Kane for so long…but love?

He rolled it around in his brain, tried to downplay it, but the truth would not be silenced. This woman had taken root in his heart. She belonged there.

Except—how? He could never tell Sara how much she meant to him, never hold her like this again, certainly never let her guess how he felt. Sara deserved so much more than he could offer.

She was going to leave here. Kyle would pretend it was for her good, because it was. Wasn't it better that she go believing that he didn't care for her than to add another burden to her already heavy load?

Kyle pushed away everything but his concern for this precious woman. She was alone. Here, now, there was no one but him to comfort her, to help her through this. He couldn't back away, he couldn't ignore her suffering. He had to do something. He lifted his hands and cupped them around her face, forcing her to look at him.

"Sara, I don't know how God soothes our deepest hurts. I don't understand how He comforts us and brings us out of the dark places," he whispered. "I only know He does. He will."

Gradually her sobs died away. When she finally lifted her head to look at him, he saw that the light that made her silver eyes glow was gone. His heart grieved that sweet Sara and her irrepressible positive outlook had been crushed.

"He will," he repeated.

"You're talking to me about God?" She tilted her head to one side. "I thought you were mad at God."

"I, um, was." He stammered to a halt, embarrassed now to realize how silly it was to think he understood God's plans. "I've been meeting with that new minister, trying to sort out some things."

"Oh, Kyle, I'm so glad that you're searching to restore your faith." She hugged him tightly. Kyle reveled in her embrace. Too soon she pulled away and straightened her apron. "Sometimes it's hard to accept God's ways, but you won't regret it. The most important thing is that you find Him again."

"That's what Rick keeps saying. Figure out the issues and work them through. The things he says have begun to strike home."

"Really? Do you mind telling me?" She waited until he was seated then sat across from him.

"No." Sharing with this woman seemed so right, so natural, that Kyle couldn't seem to help himself. "But the first thing I need to do is apologize. I hurt you and I never want to do that. I'm sorry."

"That doesn't matter. It's forgotten." She folded

her hands in her lap. "Tell me the good stuff, the stuff you've learned about God."

"Okay. Well, Rick said my dad left me a legacy that it's my duty to pass on. I never thought of it that way but he's right."

Sara gave him one of her beautiful, warm smiles, encouraging him to continue.

"The things I loved about Churchill are the same things the boys need to learn," Kyle continued. "Learning how to deal with the hardships this land presents will help them find pride in themselves and realize they aren't weak, that they don't have to be patsies for some drug pusher or gang leader." He took a deep breath. "That's why I'm going to take them on an overnight survival trek next week. I've already okayed it with Laurel. It will be my Christmas gift to them."

"Before you go, you mean." Sara's face tightened but she kept a bead on him.

"Yes." But as he studied her face, Kyle knew he couldn't leave without trying to do something that would reunite her with the brother she so longed to see again. "Sara, would you mind if I talked to Samuel?"

"Oh, Kyle, that's such a lovely offer. But I don't think it will do any good," she said, frowning. "His letter is pretty adamant about not wanting anything to do with me. Maybe it's better to respect his wishes, but thank you, Kyle."

He nodded, still listening but mulling over the possibility of contacting her brother, anyway. Maybe he could get Samuel to at least talk to her. That would make a good Christmas gift and if it didn't work out, she wouldn't be disappointed.

"I've been talking to Rick, too," she told him.

Kyle didn't have to ask why. He knew the reason Sara had sought out Rick was to soothe her hurting heart over the family God seemed disinclined to give. If ever someone deserved that family, it was Sara. He knew she was also hurting over his rejection. She'd probably told the pastor about that. Again Kyle felt ashamed of his harsh words.

"I love working here. That day we were on the snowmobile I started to think that maybe God wanted me to stay, to keep working with the boys. But I don't think that anymore."

"Why?" He couldn't fathom Lives without Sara.

"Because God's ways aren't ours and just because I want something, doesn't mean He wants it for me." Her head dipped. "I have to leave."

"What's made you so sure?" Kyle sensed something else was going on.

"God doesn't want me here because I don't deserve the privilege of staying here," she whispered.

"Why do you think that, Sara?" His heart felt as if it was squeezed in a vise.

"Because I caused Maria's death." Sara shook her head, loosening a few tendrils of hair that slid down to caress her cheek. "That's why God wants me to leave. That's why I have to be alone. I don't deserve a family."

"Sara, no. God isn't like that." He tried to make her understand what he himself had only just begun to fathom. "God's love doesn't depend on us deserving it. God gives His love freely. Even if you did make a mistake, you asked for forgiveness, didn't you?" He waited until she'd nodded. "He looks at you and loves you as His precious child. He doesn't want you to suffer."

"Then why doesn't He answer my prayer for a family?" she demanded, eyes blazing. When he couldn't answer, she smiled the saddest smile he'd ever seen. "Don't worry, Kyle, I'll live on my own and continue to serve Him. It's just that I would have loved—"

With a small, tired sigh she rose and returned to the counter, where she continued rolling out the pastry she'd begun.

Kyle opened his mouth to argue, but what could he say? He couldn't tell her what was in his heart, that he wanted to be with her forever, to make her world happy and fulfilled. Because he couldn't do that. The doctors had been clear, the shrapnel had done its damage. There was little chance that he could father a child.

Sara wanted a family, children. Lots of them.

Kyle slowly turned and left the kitchen. He went

to the family room and laid out the things he'd brought, ready to begin a survival class as soon as the boys returned from school.

But no matter how busy he kept himself, he couldn't shake the image of Sara in his arms, the light lemon fragrance of her hair filling his senses, sobbing as if her heart was breaking.

He thought again of the verse he'd read this morning in Psalms 66.

You let men ride over our heads, we went through fire and water, yet you brought us to a place of abundance.

"I'm trying to wait and let You bring me to that place of abundance," he prayed. "I'm trying to follow the directions You give."

Kyle stared out the window at the snow-covered land he loved.

"But oh, God, what am I supposed to do about Sara?"

"Two days until we go on our trek," Kyle told the boys gathered around him. "I've got a little quiz to see how ready you are."

Sara had spent the past few days listening in, pretending she wasn't paying attention as she knit a pair of mitts for Laurel. The truth was she reveled in every word Kyle said. She needed to hear the sound of his voice, to see his face come alive as he explained how to track, how to see wild animals without scaring them away, how to survive in the wilderness.

But after ten minutes Sara knew that today, for some reason, she couldn't listen anymore. It hurt too much. She had to get away. She waited until the boys huddled around the coffee table to work on their quiz.

"Can I borrow your snowmobile, Kyle?"

He frowned at her. "By yourself?" She nodded. "What for?"

"I need to get out." When he hesitated, Sara pleaded her case. "You've given me several lessons on it. I know my way around. I just want to be alone for a bit."

"Okay." He dug out his keys and handed them to her. "Don't go far," he ordered.

"Just toward town, I promise." She took his keys and hurried away.

"Sara. Can I talk to you for a minute?" Laurel watched her fasten her snow boots.

"Can it wait until I come back?"

"This won't take long." Laurel sat down across from her. "Honey, I know you said you only wanted to stay till Christmas, but are you sure? I don't have to bring the new cook out. You don't have to leave."

The choice dangled in front of her with tantalizing sweetness. Stay, see Kyle every day, see the boys change and grow.

"Laurel, I promised you I'd go before New Year's

when I came here and I'm not changing my mind. Besides," she said very quietly, "this isn't where I belong."

"Then—"

"Where will I go?" Sara smiled. "I've been wondering that myself. I think I'll go back to Vancouver for a while. Maybe there's something there God would have me do."

"Honey, are you sure?" Laurel asked.

"No, I'm not sure at all," Sara muttered. "It's like there's a block between God and me, and no matter how hard I pray, I can't get through it. I was so sure He sent me here to find my family and reunite them. I thought that was His plan for me. But I was wrong."

"Sweetie." Laurel frowned but said nothing else, as if she didn't know what to say.

"It will be hard for me to leave here." She jumped up and hugged her best friend. "I've loved every moment of my time here at Lives."

Sara couldn't say any more. It was too hard. So she zipped up her coat, pulled on her mitts and grabbed Kyle's helmet.

"Take my cell phone, just in case," Laurel urged before she could get out the door.

"Thanks." Sara stuffed it in her pocket then hurried away, anxious not to weep in front of her friend.

But once she was on the snowmobile she couldn't stop her tears. She blinked furiously, trying to see the way before her. But the deep sense of loss, the feeling of being abandoned by God in Whom she'd placed so much trust, only added to the depression engulfing her. For once the softly falling snow did nothing to heighten her mood.

As Sara drove, she couldn't dislodge the images of the boys gathered around Kyle, his face intent as he taught them. He'd found his niche. He was a born instructor. Maybe he hadn't accepted it yet, but Sara knew in her heart that Kyle would be staying in Churchill. This was his home. He belonged here.

She didn't.

Why, God? I'm in love with Kyle. I could help him. I could help the kids. Why haven't You given me my dream?

Heartbroken, Sara soon realized she'd made the very mistake Kyle had warned her of over and over. She lost track of her surroundings. Where was she? Surely that lump of white over there was familiar? She slowed the sled to a stop then surveyed the area. Nothing seemed quite where it should be.

She was lost.

Using great care, Sara turned the sled around and tried to follow her tracks back. But the snow was falling more heavily now and it was difficult to find her tracks in the white-on-white landscape.

Fear rose as she recalled the many stories she'd heard about people getting lost in the wilderness. Without meaning to, she gunned the engine. The snowmobile spurted forward in a rush of motion, hit something then swayed sideways, throwing her off. Her head hit something hard. Everything went black.

"Sara should have been back before now." Kyle glanced from his watch to Laurel's face and knew that she was as worried as he was. "Has anyone seen her?"

Laurel shook her head, her face pale.

"I'll call Teddy, get him to drive out here and check along the way." He was grateful his friend was still in town. Teddy had talked of going to his son's for Christmas. "He's coming," he said, hanging up the phone.

"I gave her my cell phone, but she doesn't answer." Laurel's eyes met his. "Something's wrong." She wrung her hands. "I should have stopped her. She was so upset when she left."

"Upset?" Kyle's radar went on high alert. "What happened?"

"I don't know. I asked her if she was sure she wouldn't stay on after Christmas and she said no, she loved it here but she had to leave. She said she didn't belong here, but she does, Kyle. I should never have accepted her resignation."

Didn't belong?

The silliness of that statement stunned Kyle. Sara Kane belonged at Lives Under Construction as much as polar bears belonged in Churchill.

She belonged to him, she was in his heart, his very soul. She made his days worthwhile. And he couldn't give her up.

"What should we do?" Laurel asked him.

Kyle glanced outside. "Even if it wasn't storming, I can't track in the dark. By morning everything will be covered. I'd go out there right now if I thought it would do any good, but running off half-cocked won't help Sara."

"Then what?" Laurel asked.

"Pray." Rod stood in the doorway. It was obvious that he'd heard their concern. "It's what Sara would do. She prays about everything. That's why she has no fear. She doesn't depend on herself, she depends on God."

The words hit their target in Kyle's heart. Sara had accused him of that before, of believing he had to rely on himself.

"Sara would tell us to trust God," Rod said.

"Out of the mouths of babes," Laurel murmured. She touched his shoulder. "I'm going to talk to the boys. I'll be back," she said, leading Rod out of the room.

Kyle looked out the window again, thinking of how he'd told Sara he was repairing his relationship with God. How far did that go? Far enough to trust God with Sara's life, no matter what? Trust God to face whatever problems might come?

That applied equally to the future. Kyle loved

Sara, he knew that with every fiber of his being. If he told her, if he accepted the love she'd so freely offered, could he trust God to help him face whatever problems would come, problems he could never handle on his own?

"Yes."

"Yes, what?" Teddy asked, standing in the doorway.

"Yes, I love Sara. Yes, I am going to trust that God will work out our future, if she'll have me. And yes, we are going to find her." He looked at his friend. "Any problem with that?"

"Not one." Teddy grinned as he clapped Kyle on the back. "What's our next move?"

"We're going to organize a search party so that when this breaks, we'll be ready to go out and find her. But first, we're going to pray. Then I have an important phone call to make for Sara."

Teddy bowed his head and led them in a prayer for safety for Sara, for clear weather and for God's leading in finding her.

"Amen." Kyle said. "Now let's get to work."

Chapter Fourteen

Sara came to with the realization that she was freezing cold. She sat up, blinked away the flakes sticking to her lashes and found she was almost buried in the snow. Her fingers and toes tingled. She rose, moving gingerly to get her circulation flowing.

She glanced around hopefully, but everything was still covered in a downy blanket, obscuring whatever landmark might lie beneath. The knowledge hit like a sledgehammer.

She could die out here.

"God, I need help," she whispered, her heart like a block of ice in her chest.

Already the sky grew darker as evening crept in. Panicked, Sara felt in her pocket for Laurel's phone, praying she could get a signal.

But the phone wasn't in her pocket.

Though she looked for it, feeling around in the snow with her hands, she could not find it.

The first sign of hypothermia will creep up on you. You must be prepared to protect yourself. If you're lost, stay put. Dig a shelter in the snow, but make sure something is visible for searchers to see. Kyle's voice from this afternoon's survival lesson filled her mind.

Sara levered her hands under the snowmobile to right it. The machine was heavy and sitting awkwardly. At first it didn't budge, but she pushed back the ache in her head, amassed all her strength and shoved. Finally the machine flopped over onto its skis.

But when she attempted to start it, nothing happened. Over and over she tried the ignition but nothing happened. The last time she tried, the battery died.

Flurries whirled around her as the wind whipped the snow. Soon it would be completely dark.

Quickly Sara scraped snow together with her mittened hands and piled it high. The slightly damp snow packed easily. She pressed it around one side of the snowmobile, using the machine as a wall of her shelter. She swept the other side of the machine clear so the black seat and silvery skis were visible.

Satisfied she'd done her best, she slid inside her snow house as the remaining flickers of light faded. Before she packed the last bit of snow around her head, she glanced left. Her breath snagged in her throat.

Two lumbering white shapes plodded through the wilderness barely two hundred feet away.

Polar bears.

"Lord, please protect me," Sara prayed, her temples throbbing. Buried as she was, she could hear the whistle of the wind and nothing else.

It seemed she sat there for hours, on edge, waiting for the bears to find her. But they, too, must have sought shelter as the wind now screamed across the land.

"I always thought I was alone before," she whispered to the only one who could hear her. "But now I am truly alone. I thought I could make up for my mistake with Maria if I worked hard at Lives, helped in the community, made it better for other people. But I see now that it doesn't work. I guess that's why You haven't shown me the future and where You want me to go—because it doesn't matter."

A new gust of wind penetrated her frail shelter. She packed more snow to block the draft. Every so often she poked her head outside. Once she thought she saw the bears sitting together, watching her, before the whirling snow blurred everything.

She thought of Kyle. How she loved him. How she wanted the best for him, health and freedom from his pain, a solidifying of his faith to total trust in God. How she wished she could stay to watch him take a leadership role at Lives, be part of his world.

She suddenly knew with every fiber of her being

that Kyle would come looking for her, and the thought of her mistake putting him at risk was more than she could bear.

Her head and her heart ached too much. Sara leaned back and let sleep overtake her.

Sara was cold, so cold.

Her lips felt cracked and frozen as she opened her eyes, with no idea of how much time had passed.

There was no sign any of her prayers had been heard. She had to let in fresh oxygen. She poked her head through the snow and immediately noticed the wind had died down. A hush enveloped the land. How light it seemed. Why?

Eyes widening, she blinked at the incredible beauty playing out in the night sky. Ribbons of misty green, turquoise, blue—oh, there were a hundred shades, and they spun and wove across the sky in the most amazing show. Because of them she could clearly see the polar bears, sitting in the same place, waiting and watching.

Then, as if a conductor had mounted the podium, the lights moved in sideways arcs so that Sara was almost encircled.

Praises rose from her heart.

In that moment truth dawned.

"I'm not alone. How could I be alone when You are all around me?" she whispered. "I am a part of Your family. You love me."

She had to be silent for a moment, to let it sink in. The lights grew more intense, more active, richer in color, mirroring the revelation bursting in her heart.

"You have loved me more than any family could have. You protected me, cared for me, brought me to a place where I could give to kids who need it so desperately. You're not asking me to leave. This is where You want me, here in Churchill, at Lives. This is where I belong." The wonder of it silenced her for a moment.

Then she thought of Kyle and her heart pinched with longing. She looked to the sky and felt heavenly reassurance. If Kyle couldn't love her, God would heal her heart. She had to trust Him to do that because Sara knew now with utmost certainty that she could not leave this place.

The lights swayed, deepening and changing color, beckoning her to full committal. Sara gazed at the heavens. *Trust,* they seemed to whisper.

Inhaling deeply, she nodded.

"I'm putting my future in Your hands, God. I love Kyle, but I'm leaving him and my brother up to You. Your will be done."

The lights rippled and swelled as profound peace filled Sara. Her dream of a family, of Kyle—all of those hopes melted away. God was her Father. He would care for her. He knew best.

A song the boys had taught her rose to her lips.

She sang it loudly, joyfully, uncaring of the bears that sat mere feet away. They, too, were God's creatures.

She had nothing to fear.

"Listen to me, Samuel. Your sister did everything she could to find you." Kyle grimaced when the other man interrupted. "Let me finish. You have no idea what Sara Kane is like, what she's gone through, why she's so desperate to see you again. I suggest you do some research online. When you read why she couldn't rescue you, perhaps you'll realize that Sara is the best sister you could ever hope to have." Kyle clicked off his phone.

"Are you sure that was wise?" Teddy asked.

"Probably not, but maybe it will help him get over his 'poor me' attitude." He frowned. "What is that racket?"

"Our volunteer force. Take a look." Teddy opened the computer room door.

Kyle gaped. Lives Under Construction bulged with people, spilling into the hallway, coming in the front door.

"Once they heard about Sara, they came. I think everyone in town is here. Everyone loves her." Teddy's face softened.

"I love her, too." Kyle checked the weather outside. It was as good as it was going to get. "Let's go talk to them," he told Teddy.

Rod got everyone's attention by whistling. Kyle smiled his thanks at the boy as silence fell.

"Folks, the storm is over for now, but weather reports say another one will start sometime later this afternoon. We have about three hours of daylight to search for Sara. I've laid out a grid pattern. We'll assign teams to each section. Have your cell phones with you and be sure they're fully charged. Now let's find Sara and bring her home. But first let's pray."

Oddly Kyle felt no hesitation about praying publicly. His certainty that he needed Sara is his life grew with every passing moment. If he had to, he would lay down his life for her. If she'd agree, he'd spend the rest of his days giving her everything he had.

He had to trust God that his everything would be enough for Sara.

At the end of Kyle's prayer, Pastor Rick added his own. Then the groups assembled and set out on their search. Teddy had set up a portable communications station in Laurel's kitchen. He quickly familiarized her with the system. The boys approached Kyle.

"We want to help search for Sara, too," Tony told him.

Kyle recognized how badly they wanted to help the woman who had so selflessly loved them. He called over one of the police officers.

"The boys want to help." He shot the officer a look that begged him to agree.

"We're going to do a search around town," the Mountie said. "We can use all the help we can get. Come with me, guys."

"Kyle?" Teddy beckoned him over. He pointed to a section on the map. "I didn't dare give this to anyone else. It's tricky to navigate and there are reports of a bear and her cub there. You're the one who knows this area the best."

"It's so far out. You think she would have gone that far?" Kyle asked, frowning as he studied the map.

Teddy's reasoning convinced him that it was possible Sara had mistaken a turn on the way into town. If she had taken the route he believed, it would take every ounce of Kyle's energy to get there and back with his leg aching as it was.

But he'd gladly do that and more to get Sara safe in his arms.

I can do all things through God, Who strengthens me. It was a promise his mom had clung to. Kyle tucked it deep inside, took a breath and nodded.

"Okay, let's go, Teddy." He grabbed his backpack, put the thermos of coffee Laurel gave him inside and zipped his snowsuit. "Pray," he begged her.

"Without ceasing," Laurel promised. She hugged him. "You bring her back."

"I intend to." Kyle set out on a borrowed machine with Teddy behind on his own. They'd need two sleds when they found Sara. Once in the open he revved the motor. Teddy followed. They raced across the land, taking a shortcut to get to the spot Teddy had marked on the map, ever aware that night was coming, fast.

After they'd gone ten miles without seeing anything unusual, Kyle stopped. He flipped the visor on his helmet to speak to Teddy.

"The marsh is ahead." He studied the ground but couldn't discern any tracks. "The machines will bog down in the weeds. I can't see anything to indicate she went in there. You?"

Teddy shook his head. "Nothing."

"The wind's picking up." Wind chill made the temperature dangerously frigid. Kyle checked his watch, grimaced. *Too long, God. It's taking too long.*

"It'll get colder now with the sky clearing," his friend noted. "Do you think Sara could read the night sky enough to navigate by it?"

"I doubt it." Kyle squeezed his eyes closed and summoned her lovely face to mind. *Dear Sara.* The image warmed him until he remembered the bear warning. "Sara's a city girl. I don't think she'd know much about survival out here." Panic reached down and squeezed his stomach into a knot. "What am I going to do if—"

"Don't give up." Teddy bowed his head. "God, we need help here."

Kyle silently added his pleas to the prayer but was interrupted when he lifted his head and suddenly gave a shout. Kyle strained to follow Teddy's pointing finger. Ahead of them, just to the right, the aurora borealis flashed an arc of incredible silvergreen through the sky then undulated like an unfurling ribbon, lighting the ground ahead of them.

"Forward," Teddy murmured. He pulled down his visor.

Kyle said nothing, his focus on the land around them, his heart praying. The northern lights continued to shift, swelling and heaving, ever changing. Kyle had never seen them so bright.

But he saw no sign of Sara.

Dispirited, defeated and wondering if he'd run out of favors from God, Kyle stopped to stretch his leg. It ached abominably from being bent for so long. He knew he could not last much longer on the machine. Doggedly, he revved his engine and continued his search across the frozen taiga.

His thoughts went to his last meeting with Rick. They'd talked over a verse in Psalms 69, which Rick said David had written in the deepest hours of his distress.

For Jehovah hears the cries of his needy ones and does not look the other way.

"Please look my way, God. Please help," he kept repeating as he drove. *Where are you, Sara?*

Suddenly Kyle blinked. He took a second look then stopped his machine. Teddy followed suit.

Straight ahead, two polar bears sat as if transfixed.

Kyle couldn't understand why they stayed. All at once Sara's voice, cracked with strain but filled with determination, broke through the silence of the night as she belted out "Our God Reigns."

His heart bursting with joy, Kyle climbed off his machine and tramped through the snow, following Sara's voice, afraid to drive any closer lest he crush her refuge. Moments later he saw the black leather corner of the snowmobile seat jutting out of the snow and the tip of one ski.

"Sara! Where are you?"

Seconds later the hood of Sara's bright red jacket poked through the snow. "Kyle?"

He got down in front of her, digging madly, freeing her from the snow. With tender fingers he touched the blue spot on her temple then brushed his lips against it.

"Oh, Sara, you scared me to death. Are you all right? What happened?" He listened to her story, unable to stop touching her to assure she was unhurt.

"I'm fine." She smiled. Was there anything sweeter than Sara Kane's smile?

No longer able to stop himself, Kyle folded her into his arms.

"I love you, Sara," he whispered before he covered her lips with his.

For one stunned moment she didn't move. But

the next second she had her arms around his neck. Her lips melted warm against his, returning his embrace, telling him everything he needed to know. She still loved him.

In the background, Kyle vaguely heard Teddy radioing that they'd found her, but he ignored it, awed that God had given him the desire of his heart. After a moment, Sara went very still.

"I'm pretty cold and my brain's not functioning perfectly," she murmured, tilting her head away, a frown on her face. "But did you say you love me, Kyle?"

"For ages, with all my heart, as deeply as a man can love a woman, yes," he said, kissing her between each phrase. "I love you, Sara."

"Then why did you push me away?" she demanded, her eyes showing her hurt.

"I'm sorry I did that. But I didn't think I had any other choice until God showed me a few things. We have a lot to talk about, sweetheart." He helped her up. "But it's going to have to wait until we get you home. Have a sip of Laurel's coffee. It will warm you for the ride home." He glanced at the bears that looked on with interest but hadn't moved. "Think they'll follow us?" he asked Teddy.

"Of course they won't." Sara grinned. "I can't carry a tune in a bucket. That's what kept them back there. They're well rid of me."

Teddy burst out laughing. Because her legs

seemed wobbly, he and Kyle helped her onto Kyle's sled. Then Teddy pulled him aside.

"You're in pain. You don't have to drive back. We could get a chopper out here," he said.

"I am driving Sara home," Kyle told him, daring him to argue.

Teddy studied him for a moment then smiled. "So what are we waiting for?"

"Nothing. I have all I need." Kyle glanced at Sara then headed for Churchill. He was aware of the rising wind and the snowflakes that now fell in thick sheets, but felt no fear.

"They were so beautiful," Sara murmured when they arrived at Lives and she climbed off the sled.

"What were?" Kyle slung his arm around her waist, supporting her.

"The northern lights. God gave me my own private viewing." She laid her head on his shoulder. "I love you, Kyle. I don't have to search for my family anymore."

"No, you don't, my dearest Sara. We'll be each other's family." Kyle knew the others were waiting but he was loath to let her go, until she shivered. "Inside. We'll talk later."

"You'll be here?" she asked very softly.

"Whenever you want, for as long as you want, I will be here, Sara."

But as he watched her disappear into the throng

of people waiting, Kyle wondered if she'd want him to stay when she learned the truth and realized he couldn't give her the family she craved.

Chapter Fifteen

Snuggled in a big, fluffy quilt, which Lucy insisted on, Sara turned so she was leaning against the sofa arm, facing Kyle. She looked into his eyes and knew he was struggling to tell her something.

"Did you mean what you said?" she asked, glad they were finally alone in the big family room.

"Which part?" He looked at her then smiled. "Of course I love you. Couldn't you tell?"

"No," she said simply. "As you said, I don't know anything about loving someone."

"Oh, Sara, don't repeat my stupidity. I was wrong and so are you. You know all about love. You've taught all of us—the boys, folks in town, me." He took her hands in his and brought them to his lips. "You've taught us all the true meaning of love. You go above and beyond for everyone. You refuse to take no for an answer. That's why I love you so much."

"But—" Sara struggled to put the pieces together

in her mind. "If you loved me, why did you tell me you didn't? Would you have let me leave knowing that you loved me?"

"If God hadn't shaken me up?" He shook his head. "Truthfully, I don't know. I was so stubborn, so determined not to depend on anyone." He grimaced. "I was afraid."

Sara studied their entwined fingers and wondered. Was her love enough for him? Maybe he'd realize she couldn't be the kind of woman he wanted.

"Sara." He bent forward so she had to look at him. "Why do you think I've turned down three offers on the house? The last couple offered way more than my asking price but I made up an excuse not to sell because I couldn't leave you." A fierce look filled his face. "I promise I'll do my best not to lean on you too much and I will relearn how to do as much as God wants me to."

Her heart melted at his declaration. God had answered her deepest prayers. Sara flung her arms around his neck.

"My darling Kyle, we'll each have to lean on the other, and God." She kissed him then leaned back. "I come with a lot of baggage, Kyle. You're going to need patience."

"Not a hardship as long as you have patience with me." He hugged her. "Sara, I need to tell you something else."

"Okay." Worried by the grave tone of his voice, she drew back.

"Before this goes any further I have to say this." He inhaled then spoke. "One of the reasons I pushed you away is because I can't have kids. The doctors said my injuries make that almost impossible."

His words came out slowly. Sara sat frozen, absorbing everything he said. To never have her own child—no! She squeezed her eyes closed and prayed and once more the soft, sweet assurance rushed in. God was in charge and He would fill her life with joy.

"I know how much you want a family of your own," Kyle murmured. He tried to hide it but his face showed how much it cost him to tell her the truth. "I can't give you that. All I have to offer you is love."

Tears came to her eyes. *All he had to offer.* As if she was somehow getting second best with this loving, tender man who had risked his life for her.

"If you want to change your mind—"

She stopped his speech with the simple gesture of leaning over and covering his lips with hers. She kissed him as deeply, as passionately as she knew how, pouring her heart and soul into it. And wonder of wonders, Kyle kissed her back. When she finally pulled away she was breathless.

"I already have a family, Kyle. A huge one. Laurel, the boys, this town, Lucy and Hector. You. Especially you." She snuggled her head against his chest. "God has blessed me so richly."

"Are you still leaving, Sara? I'll live wherever you want to. We'll start over together." He blinked at the smile that lifted her lips. "What?"

"I'm not leaving Churchill, Kyle. I can't." She grasped both his hands in her small ones and explained. "Out in the snow I figured out what God wants for my future." She spread her hands wide. "Churchill is my home, Kyle. This is where God wants me, here at Lives, in town, in the church, helping out wherever I can. I couldn't help Maria. But I can help the boys who come here. That's what God wants."

"I'm certainly glad to hear that." Laurel stepped into the room. "Sorry to interrupt you two but I just discovered that our new cook isn't as accomplished as I'd expected. She's worried about taking on everything here and asked if someone would train her. As head cook, Sara, you could do that. We'll need help if my plan to expand goes ahead. Is that something you're interested in?"

"Head cook? Yes! Yes, yes, yes." Sara jumped up and hugged her boss. "I'd love to stay." She twirled around, her heart full of thanksgiving for the plans God had for her.

"Okay, then." Laurel smiled. "We'll talk in the morning. I'll leave you two alone now."

Sara flopped down on the couch, exhausted but

so happy. "I'm so happy I can stay here. But knowing you're completely reconciled with God is the best thing of all."

"Yes, it is," he agreed, caressing her arm.

"What changed that for you?" she whispered, her fingers threading with his, loving the way he drew her close.

"Realizing that I couldn't keep you safe. It didn't matter what I did. I was powerless to get you home. I had to rely on someone else, on a whole lot of others. Finally I had to rely on God to show us where you were." He brushed his lips against her forehead then sighed. "That was so hard."

"Why?" she asked.

"Ever since I got hurt, I've had to depend on others in some way, shape or form. And I hated it. It made me feel like I was a loser. My doubts about my future magnified." He squeezed her shoulder. "But then there you were, pushing your way into my life and forcing me to care for you. How could I not love you?"

"I love you, too, Kyle. So much." Sara tipped her head up to receive his kiss. "God has answered so many of my prayers it's like Christmas has come early. What else could I possibly want?"

"Well." Kyle's eyes, blue whorls of uncertainty, rested on her. "I haven't got a job, Sara. I don't know if I can stay here or what I'd do. I was going to open a computer store in Winnipeg but—"

"I believe God has more important things for you to do, Kyle." Sara slid her arms around his waist and laid her head on his shoulder. "The boys that are here and the ones yet to come need you to teach them how to be men of integrity. God blessed you with wonderful parents so you can pass on the lessons they taught you. That's why He saved you in Afghanistan. That's why He led you back here. He'll work it out, Kyle. Just have some faith."

"You're going to be a wonderful partner, Sara Kane." Kyle drew his arms around her and showed her how much he needed her in his world. "So when should we get married?"

"But—" Marry him? Her heart stopped. She stared at him, thrilled by the thought of spending the rest of her life with this wonderful man.

"What? You don't want to marry me?" Kyle teased, playing with a tendril of her hair. But there was the tiniest doubt in his voice.

"Yes, I want to marry you. But you never asked me."

A moment later Kyle was kneeling in front of her, holding her hands and staring into her eyes.

"My dearest Sara, will you please marry me? I have no job, my house is on the market and I have no idea how I will support you. But I'm willing to trust God for what we need."

Trust Kyle to make sure he'd covered all the bases with his proposal. How she loved this man.

"Yes, Kyle. I will gladly marry you, because I love you."

She tilted her head to kiss him just as his phone rang, making them both laugh.

He spoke into it for a few moments, assured the caller that Sara was fine then handed the phone to her. "Someone wants to speak with you."

"Hello," she said.

"This is Samuel. Kyle called me. I was wondering if we might talk sometime."

Sara slumped into Kyle's tender embrace and closed her eyes.

"Sara?" the phone squeaked.

"Sorry," she apologized, staring into Kyle's loving eyes. "I just needed a minute to thank God."

"For what?" her brother asked.

"For giving me two wonderful men in my family." She laughed when Samuel said she might be making a mistake about him. "No. God brought you both into my life," she told him, staring into Kyle's rich, blue eyes. "And God doesn't make mistakes. Not ever."

Epilogue

On a warm July day the entire town of Churchill gathered on the windswept cliffs overlooking Hudson Bay for the wedding of Sara Kane to their own Kyle Loness. White tulle draped around an arch billowed in the breeze where Kyle, resplendent in his military uniform, waited for his bride with his friend Teddy and Pastor Rick.

Yellow wildflowers scattered blooms over the ground between rows of white chairs where guests waited. Then the jubilant tones of the wedding march brought Laurel down the aisle. Dressed in a pale blue dress, carrying a bundle of flowers the boys had picked an hour earlier, she led the way to Kyle then stepped aside.

Sara took a deep breath but before she could move, a deep voice asked, "May I give my sister away?"

She could only nod and cling to Samuel's strong

arm as they walked slowly toward Kyle. Her groom grinned at her brother, obviously in on the surprise, but Kyle's gaze stayed locked on Sara. She handed the pale pink roses Rod had grown in Kyle's greenhouse to Laurel then took Kyle's outstretched hands. Together they faced Rick, who gave a short homily on marriage before asking for their vows.

"Sara, I promise to love you with all my heart for as long as we live. You are my sun, my moon and my northern lights. I will love you forever." Kyle slid a solid gold band onto her finger, right next to the diamond he'd given her at Christmas.

"Kyle, you are a precious gift from God. I promise to love you. Always. Forever. As long as we live." Sara placed a hammered gold band on his ring finger.

"Kyle, you may kiss your bride."

As Kyle embraced his new wife, the boys whistled and the crowd clapped. The bride and groom walked back down the aisle. Amidst a shower of birdseed, they invited everyone to join them at Lives Under Construction for the reception.

"This probably isn't what Laurel had in mind for this place, is it?" Kyle asked Sara, smiling at the decorations their friends had strung everywhere.

"It's better." She kissed his cheek. "Congratulations on your new position as activities coordinator for Lives."

"There are going to be some changes," he told her. "New boys will be arriving."

"That can wait. You and I have a honeymoon." She threw her arms around his neck. "I'm going to love Hawaii."

"I'm going to love you, forever, always." Kyle embraced her, only pulling free when Laurel insisted they had to leave for the train. A procession followed them to the old depot and the entire community gave them a send-off.

As the train chugged away Sara sent a text message to Laurel.

"What's that about?" Kyle asked.

"I just told her North Country heroes make the best husbands." She grinned at him.

"Is Laurel looking for a husband?" he asked.

"Not yet. But I've turned it over to God." She chuckled at his droll look.

"Then Teddy doesn't stand a chance."

* * * * *

Dear Reader,

Welcome to Churchill. I hope you've enjoyed this first installment in my newest miniseries, Northern Lights. Sara has faced much hardship and pain in her life. In Churchill she finds solace in pouring her heart full of love over six needy boys. Likewise, Kyle returns home to the only sanctuary he knows while he struggles to find the answers he craves. These two hearts need a master touch to bring healing and open them to love, and the great white north is just the place they'll find it. Please look for Pastor Rick's story in the second book of Northern lights, coming in 2014.

Until we meet again, may you find the peace and comfort only our Father can offer. May you know His love in the depths of your soul and may you share that love with those He sends your way.

Blessings to you, dear friend.

Love,

Questions for Discussion

1. Sara's horrific childhood left her certain she isn't worthy of love. Discuss issues others in her situation might have.

2. Kyle struggled to understand why God let his parents die, and why he lost his leg. What advice would you have given him?

3. Laurel was Sara's mother figure. Do you have someone like her in your life? What role does Laurel play as Sara deals with her past?

4. The boys who come to Lives Under Construction arrive with many problems. Would you be comfortable with such a project in your community? Discuss biases that might confront kids in such a situation.

5. Kyle felt diminished because of his injury. Do you think this is a common feeling among amputees? How would you help him deal with his need for independence?

6. Sara craved a family of her own. Spend some time considering the role of families beyond the simple nurturing aspect, such as the value of a sense of history, common goals, etc.

7. Do you think Sara's feelings of unworthiness are common? Do you struggle with them yourself? Consider ways we can make others feel valued and help them understand the depth of God's love.

8. Why do you think Sara is so certain she must leave Churchill to honor God's will? Do you ever feel God can't use you exactly where you are?

9. Once Kyle was able to break out of his self-imposed solace, he began to appreciate that others needed him. Discuss ways we can enrich our lives by extending ourselves and giving our time, attention or goods to others.

10. Sara believed she had few talents. Do you feel that way? Consider things you can do and whether these might be used to brighten another's world.

11. Churchill is a small, isolated community. Do you think its community spirit comes from the isolation or from the need to depend on your neighbor? Discuss ways you could build community spirit in your own community.

12. Sara was able to realize God's will only when she was alone in the wilderness, far from everything. When have you felt closest to God?

LARGER-PRINT BOOKS!

GET 2 FREE
LARGER-PRINT NOVELS
PLUS 2 FREE
MYSTERY GIFTS

Love Inspired

Larger-print novels are now available...

YES! Please send me 2 FREE LARGER-PRINT Love Inspired® novels and my 2 FREE mystery gifts (gifts are worth about $10). After receiving them, if I don't wish to receive any more books, I can return the shipping statement marked "cancel." If I don't cancel, I will receive 6 brand-new novels every month and be billed just $5.24 per book in the U.S. or $5.74 per book in Canada. That's a savings of at least 23% off the cover price. It's quite a bargain! Shipping and handling is just 50¢ per book in the U.S. and 75¢ per book in Canada.* I understand that accepting the 2 free books and gifts places me under no obligation to buy anything. I can always return a shipment and cancel at any time. Even if I never buy another book, the two free books and gifts are mine to keep forever.

122/322 IDN F49Y

Name	(PLEASE PRINT)	

Address		Apt. #

City	State/Prov.	Zip/Postal Code

Signature (if under 18, a parent or guardian must sign)

Mail to the Harlequin® Reader Service:
IN U.S.A.: P.O. Box 1867, Buffalo, NY 14240-1867
IN CANADA: P.O. Box 609, Fort Erie, Ontario L2A 5X3

**Are you a current subscriber to Love Inspired books
and want to receive the larger-print edition?
Call 1-800-873-8635 or visit www.ReaderService.com.**

* Terms and prices subject to change without notice. Prices do not include applicable taxes. Sales tax applicable in N.Y. Canadian residents will be charged applicable taxes. Offer not valid in Quebec. This offer is limited to one order per household. Not valid for current subscribers to Love Inspired Larger-Print books. All orders subject to credit approval. Credit or debit balances in a customer's account(s) may be offset by any other outstanding balance owed by or to the customer. Please allow 4 to 6 weeks for delivery. Offer available while quantities last.

Your Privacy—The Harlequin® Reader Service is committed to protecting your privacy. Our Privacy Policy is available online at www.ReaderService.com or upon request from the Harlequin Reader Service.

We make a portion of our mailing list available to reputable third parties that offer products we believe may interest you. If you prefer that we not exchange your name with third parties, or if you wish to clarify or modify your communication preferences, please visit us at www.ReaderService.com/consumerschoice or write to us at Harlequin Reader Service Preference Service, P.O. Box 9062, Buffalo, NY 14269. Include your complete name and address.

LILPDIR13R

ReaderService.com

Manage your account online!

- Review your order history
- Manage your payments
- Update your address

---

*We've designed
the Harlequin® Reader Service
website just for you.*

Enjoy all the features!

- Reader excerpts from any series
- Respond to mailings and special monthly offers
- Discover new series available to you
- Browse the Bonus Bucks catalog
- Share your feedback

Visit us at:

ReaderService.com

RS13

LARGER-PRINT BOOKS!

GET 2 FREE
LARGER-PRINT NOVELS
PLUS 2 FREE
MYSTERY GIFTS

Love Inspired®

SUSPENSE
RIVETING INSPIRATIONAL ROMANCE

Larger-print novels are now available...